WIDESHOES THE ANGEL

SUSAN HARDWICK

Illustrated by
Fred Chevalier

An imprint of Kevin Mayhew

First published in 1997 by
KEVIN MAYHEW LTD
Rattlesden
Bury St Edmunds
Suffolk IP30 0SZ

0 1 2 3 4 5 6 7 8 9

ISBN 0 86209 980 3
Catalogue No 1500105

Illustrations by Fred Chevalier
Typesetting by Louise Hill
Printed and bound in Finland by WSOY – Book Printing Division

CONTENTS

For Abigail and Dean

CHAPTER 1

Hattie Arrives

Wideshoes was fed-up. Nothing seemed to be going right today. Whatever she did, she managed to put her foot in it – and it was *still* only midmorning.

Wideshoes stuck her legs straight out in front of her, and surveyed her footwear critically. She loved her boots with a single-minded devotion, but they didn't exactly help – not when you were someone like her.

She sighed, lay back on the soft cloud and, with her hands clasped behind her head, gazed dreamily up at the blue, blue sky above. This was her special place; no one else knew of it.

'Wideshoes!'

Wideshoes started in dismay. She recognised that voice only too well: it was the Senior Angel in Charge of Cherubs, or Sacc as she was known to Wideshoes and the other young angels. Hers and Wideshoes' paths had already crossed today, and it had not been the best of encounters. What *had* she 'done wrong' *now*?

She peered cautiously over the edge of the

hollow in which she was lying. It was a mistake.

'Ah! *There* you are!' Sacc's wings whirred to a stop, as she landed elegantly on the side of Wideshoes' cloud, and then folded themselves neatly into place.

'I have been looking for you everywhere. Didn't you hear me calling you? Never mind . . .' She cut short Wideshoes' muttered excuses with a small wave of her hand. 'We have a bit of an emergency, and I need your help. Oh, Wideshoes, just *look* at the state of you!' Sacc sighed, then smiled. 'Still, there is no time for you to get tidied up now. You'll have to do.'

Mystified, Wideshoes followed Sacc as she swooped through the air, and landed on Celestial Cloud Nine, the receiving point for new arrivals in heaven. The young cherubs were not usually allowed here: it was considered far too sensitive an area. Wideshoes looked around her with interest and curiosity.

A moment later, there was a burst of light, and a young girl about Wideshoes' age appeared. She was alternately rubbing her eyes, and then gazing around her in a very bewildered way.

She looked at Wideshoes. 'Where *am* I?' she asked, frowning.

Sacc stepped forward, placed her arm around the girl's shoulders, and smiled. 'You are in heaven,' she said. 'And this is Wideshoes. She has been given the special task of looking after you and of making you feel at home here.'

'I *have?*' Wideshoes could scarcely believe her ears. Normally, only senior cherubs were given such an important job. She smiled brightly at the new arrival.

'Hi!' she said cheerily.

The girl stared back at Wideshoes' wild mass of curly brown hair, the dented halo perched at a precarious angle over one eye, the leggings, bootsocks folded over the top of her boots, the t-shirt, and colourful overshirt. She looked up at Sacc doubtfully, who smiled down at her. 'You go with Wideshoes. She will take care of you, and I'll see you later.'

Wideshoes held out her hand. Reluctantly, it was taken.

Wideshoes led her charge down Celestial Cloud Nine's Starlight Boulevard. She looked sideways at Sarah's pretty face which was framed by hair braided into many plaits, and with beads woven into the strands. On top was perched a hat with a curled-up brim.

'Wish I could wear *my* hair like that,' she said. 'It's *ace!*'

Sarah didn't reply, and they walked on a bit further.

Wideshoes tried to think of something else to say.

Suddenly, Sarah gave a little hop, skip and jump – then giggled. '*Awesome!* It seems ever such ages since I could do that,' she said. 'I wasn't really able to, not when I was ill. Mum and Dad

. . . they'd be *amazed* if they could see me now.'

Then her face clouded, and her smile was replaced by tears that trickled down her face and splashed onto her denim shirt. 'Mum and Dad. Will I see them again? They'll miss me so much. I *wish* they could see me now – all better . . . It was my birthday today too . . . I wonder . . . Are they . . .' The murmured, half-finished sentences hung in the air.

' *'course* you'll see 'em again.' Wideshoes jigged from one foot to the other, chewing her lip and thinking. 'Hang on. Back in a sec. Things to do. People to see. Forgot to tell Sacc some'ing.' She rushed off, returning a moment later. 'C'mon. We're going Rainbowing. We'd better get the others first, else they'll be cross if we don't.'

Sarah wiped the tears away with her sleeve, curiosity overcoming her sadness for the moment. 'Others? What others? – *Rainbowing*? What's that?'

'The Gang. Rainbowing's *ace*! You'll see.' Wideshoes looked sideways at Sarah and her irrepressible grin dimpled her cheeks. 'We'll call you Hattie, 'cause of your hat. We all have nicknames in my Gang. C'mon. Come 'n' meet them.'

9

CHAPTER 2

'Meet the Gang'

A few minutes later they arrived at a cluster of bushes covered with a mass of the blossomiest yellow and cream blossom Hattie had ever seen.

'Everything here seems like that,' Hattie thought. 'Kind of *more* than I've ever known before.' The colours were brighter and clearer, yet strangely did not dazzle or hurt her eyes. The perfume of the flowers and plants, many strange and exotic and the like of which she had never seen before, were stronger yet more delicate. The grass underfoot felt like velvet. And the things that sort of looked like trees – Wideshoes had called them telinths – seemed so solid and big yet, at the same time, soft and fragile and very beautiful with their many-coloured leaves that caught the sunlight and glittered and sparkled and shone. Wideshoes held back one side of the bush to expose an opening in the slope behind and then, on hands and knees, crawled through it.

Hattie followed, through a small passage and into a large area which seemed carved out of the slope behind. She stood up and looked round.

Overhead, small branches of nearby telinths had been woven and tied together to make a roof, and then covered with something transparent to make a watertight shelter. The telinth leaves shone like disco-lights, their reflections sending the different colours dancing around as the foliage moved in the breeze. Through the gaps the sun shone making rippling patterns on everything.

Mobiles and windchimes moved and tinkled, and some rather wonky shelves held packets of food, cans of drink, and a variety of bits and pieces. Every available gap on the walls had pictures, collages, and a great range of other works of art and imagination.

Three pairs of eyes regarded her with surprise and curiosity.

'This is Hattie,' announced Wideshoes to the owners of the eyes, and waving her hand at Hattie. 'And this is the Gang,' she continued, this time waving her hand at the three sitting there.

''otcha!'

''lo!'

'Hi!'

said the owners of the three pairs of eyes.

'Hello,' responded Hattie shyly.

'This is Tictoc,' said Wideshoes, waving her hand yet again at a tall, skinny, dreamy-looking twelve-year-old lad. He had slanted, oval-shaped, dark eyes, floppy straight dark brown hair which he now ran his fingers through – in what Hattie was to come to know as a regular gesture – and a halo worn straight round his head like a sweatband. 'He's called Tictoc, 'cause he makes that noise with his tongue when he's thinking of his latest invention. He's ever so clever, and always inventing things.'

'Which don't usually work,' chortled a second lad.

'That's Wishbone,' said Wideshoes. 'He couldn't invent anything, he's so busy clowning around. He's all musicy 'part from that.'

Hattie looked at the spiky red hair, freckles, cheery grin and laughing green eyes of the ten-year-old. Onto his belt there were clipped or hooked a wide variety of useful objects. A battered flute was stuck through at an angle. In contrast to Wideshoes, his halo was placed so far on the back of his head that it seemed a minor miracle it managed to stay on at all.

Now he took it off, grabbed Tictoc's before he could stop him, and began juggling with them, singing as he did so,

''attie! – oh,
'attie's 'ere.
She's jus' come
t' be one
of us –
oh, yeah!'

'Told you,' said Wideshoes. She turned to the third pair of eyes, which were an amazingly vivid blue, surmounted by white-blond hair over which a halo glistened. 'This is Speck. He's called Speck, 'cause of the way he talks – and 'cause he's the littlest. He's eight.'

Hattie looked down at the serious face. 'He looks just like an angel,' she thought, forgetting that was what he actually was.

'Hattie's going to be one of our gang – O.K.?' declared Wideshoes. 'And I'm taking her Rainbowing,' she continued without waiting for an answer. 'Coming?'

Before long, Wideshoes, Wishbone, Tictoc, Speck and Hattie had arrived at the Cele-Pad.

Hattie's eyes widened at the sight of the large number of brightly painted and decorated powerful helicopters that were neatly lined up. Each Celecopter had CELESTIAL AIRWAYS in bold print on its side. The Gang scrambled up the ladder into one of the Celecopters, followed by the pilot who pulled the door shut behind him. The great blades whirred slowly, then more and more quickly. Soon they were airborne, and swooping through the heavens at great speed.

'Why d'you need Celecopters if you've all got wings?' Hattie whispered.

'I 'spect it'd take heaps 'n' heaps 'n' *heaps* of

time to fly all over the sky. It's *ever* so huge,' said Speck.

''sides which, we'd get ever so tired using our own wings all the time. We need our energy for more 'portant things,' Wideshoes added. She pointed out of the window. 'Look!'

Hattie gasped in amazement at the vivid blaze of colours first one shade, then another, then another, that filled her vision. Great arcs of red, orange, yellow, green, blue, indigo and violet – each glowing colour clearly defined – stretched past them and out of sight. The inside of the Celecopter was lit up like a twirling kaleidoscope with the dancing vibrant colours.

'It's *beautiful*! What is it?'

'It's a rainbow, 'course! Haven't you never seen one before?'

'You wouldn't remember, Wideshoes, but they look very different from down below to people on Earth,' the pilot said. 'If she has only just arrived Hattie would never have seen one close to before.' He brought the Celecopter expertly down on to the landing pad then jumped out, followed by the Gang. 'Have fun,' he smiled. He climbed back on board, the great blades began to rotate, and the Gang watched the Celecopter lift off and whirl out of sight, the sun reflecting brightly from the multi-coloured bodywork.

'C'mon! Wotcha 'angin' 'bout for?' Wishbone set off doing a series of cartwheels, with Speck skipping and hopping along beside him. Tictoc dawdled behind making notes on a pad, his brow furrowed. He was planning another invention, and he just couldn't get the calculations right. It was all very frustrating.

Hattie ran to catch Wideshoes up. 'What d'he mean about "you wouldn't remember"? How long've you been here?'

'Mmm . . . Not sure . . . *Heaps* of time,' said Wideshoes vaguely. 'We were told at school that time here's different from time on Earth. I was *really* little when I came.'

'What d'you mean "time's different"?'

'Well . . . Our teacher said that a lot of people on Earth never seem to have 'nough time to do what they really want to do. 'n' that they're always rushing around being busy doing things they *don't* 'ticularly want to do. Well, here there's always *loads* of time to do what's 'portant. Like Rainbowing, f'rinstance.'

Hattie had lots more questions she wanted

to ask, but they had arrived at an enclosed area filled with people of all ages. There was a holiday atmosphere, and everyone was chattering and laughing. The Gang wove their way through the throng, until they were at a wide platform. People in rainbow-coloured single-suits were seating those queuing into sledges.

'Hi!' one of the young helpers greeted Wishbone, as he cartwheeled up. 'You O.K.? – Who's this?'

Wishbone introduced Hattie, then they climbed aboard one of the sledges. After a brief argument Tictoc sat in front with Hattie. Wishbone and Wideshoes sat behind, with Speck squashed in between, and they were all strapped in.

The sledge was bright red. The front curled up and over like a wave about to break on the seashore. The sides also curved up and over in the same way, but not so high. In front of each of them was a bar on which to cling.

Tictoc chewed his pencil, and jotted a few more figures down. Speck wriggled with joyous anticipation.

Wishbone noticed. 'Why y' wrigglin?' he asked suspiciously. 'You *did* "go" before . . .?'

Speck nodded happily, ''course,' he said, and wriggled again.

'You'd better 've,' warned Wishbone.

The rainbow stretched and curved away in front of them, for what seemed forever, and then out of sight. Hattie gulped nervously.

CHAPTER 3

Rainbowing and the Jacey Challenge

'Are we . . . are we . . . going . . . all the way? Down there?' Hattie asked in a small voice. 'How much – how much further does it go beyond that bend? How do we get back?'

'Don't *worry*! It's O.K. Really, *reeelly* it is.' Wideshoes' face was alight with excitement.

'Yeah!' said Wishbone. 'It's *ace*. You'll love it!'

Hattie wasn't too sure about that. She had been on rollercoasters before, but that was on Earth and *they* paled into insignificance beside *this*. She was just about to say, ever so casually, that she'd watch from the platform and wait for them to come back, when the sledge began to move. Slowly at first, then faster and faster.

Tictoc sighed, and put away notepad and pencil. He'd have to finish those calculations some other time.

Hattie gripped the bar in front of her. She shut her eyes tight, then, a moment later, opened them just a fraction. Although they were by now skimming at an immense speed down the

middle of the rainbow, it was so smooth that it didn't feel as scary as she thought it would.

She opened her eyes a bit more. Her fear began to slip away, and she realised she was enjoying herself.

The green strip on which they were travelling seemed as though it had invisible runners that kept the sledge in the middle. On one side stretched the red, orange and yellow stripes of the rainbow and, on the other, were the blue and indigo and violet. Everywhere seemed to be filled with the beautiful, glowing colours, which glistened and shone and danced in the midday sun.

'Oh, yeah! Oh, yeah!' shouted Wishbone at the top of his voice.

Speck squealed with delight, and even Tictoc grinned with pleasure as the sledge swept round a rainbow curve.

'Wheeee!' shrieked Wideshoes.

'Wow-oh-wow-oh-*wow*!' whooped Hattie ecstatically, head flung back, and beaded hair flying in the wind.

Time seemed to stand still as they banked first this way, then that, following the curve of the rainbow. They saw an aeroplane in the distance, and waved and whooped at it. The plane dipped its wings, though whether at them, or for some other reason, they were not sure.

The pilot in the aircraft switched on the passenger intercom. 'Ladies and gentlemen,' he announced. 'I apologise for the unsteadiness of the plane these last few moments, but we have been passing through some air turbulence. However, we are through it now, and I hope you won't be disturbed again.'

'Look, Sam!' said one passenger to her young son. 'What a beautiful rainbow.'

Sam looked up from his mini-computer game, and glanced briefly out of the window. 'Boring,' he said, then returned to his game.

Meanwhile, the Rainbow Sledge continued on its breakneck-speed journey with the exultant Gang on board.

At times, they disappeared into the soft white or grey mist of clouds which gently wrapped themselves around the cherubs and their craft, enclosing them in a cocoon of silence and making it feel as if they were the only people in all the universe.

Eventually, the sledge began to slow down, and then finally drew smoothly to a halt. More willing hands were there to help them undo their straps, and step shakily out.

'Oh! – *Wow!*' gasped Hattie, breathless with the speed at which they had been going, and all that she had seen. Her legs felt a bit wobbly, and she plonked down onto the ground.

'Hiya!' It was Jacko, a cherub of their age, who swooped down, slowing at the very last possible moment, and then skidding to a halt with a very realistic imitation of screeching brakes. 'I've bin lookin' everywhere for you lot. Roulus wants to see *all* the Midi Cherubs 'bout the Jacey Challenge. C'mon. Hurry up!'

A lot of the others were already there, and were chattering excitedly when Jacko, Wideshoes and Gang arrived at the Great Space. More children crowded in.

'Look, Wideshoes,' said Wishbone, nudging her. 'Goodie 'n' Co.'

Wideshoes glanced over. 'Huh!' she sniffed.

Goodie was Wideshoes' Problem Relationship and Arch-rival – and Wideshoes was Goodie's. Everything about the two seemed different as different could be.

Whereas Wideshoes was always getting into scrapes of one kind or another, Goodie never did. Whereas Wideshoes' wild brown curls seemed to have a mind and life of their own, Goodie's long golden locks lay straight and brushed and gleaming.

Goodie's shoes were small and well polished, and her dress dainty and elegant – whereas Wideshoes favoured leggings or jeans, boot-socks folded over her beloved boots, t-shirts and overshirts and her other beloved possession, her denim jacket.

Goodie's perfectly placed halo gleamed golden and shiny over her golden and shiny hair – whereas Wideshoes preferred to wear hers at a rakish and precarious angle, and so it was always falling off and getting dented.

Goodie sensed Wishbone's and Wideshoes' gaze upon her, and she turned and gave them a superior smile. She had obviously, as usual, spent a great deal of care with her appearance and every aspect of her gleamed. Now she looked Wideshoes up and down, smiled again, then turned to say something to her friend, who giggled.

'Ooh!' said Wideshoes crossly, unable to find the words to express her feelings.

At that moment the whole area suddenly

hushed. Hattie turned to where everyone's attention was directed, then gasped.

Standing at the front, and facing them all, was a giant. He must have been at least three metres in height, with olive-coloured skin, and mighty wings that looked powerful enough to take him anywhere in the heavens. A mass of dark hair curled into his neck, and dark flashing eyes scanned the assembled cherubs. An expressive mouth now curved into a merry smile. He looked strong enough to do anything – just like Samson in the Bible, Hattie thought.

'Who *is* he?' she whispered in awe to Wishbone.

'Roulus. 'e's our special Archangel. You know – f'the cherubs. 'e sorta looks out f'r us.

Roulus thanked them all for coming, then talked lightheartedly for a few minutes about this and that, and making the assembled cherubs laugh at what he said. His voice was deep and strong, a bit like rumbling thunder, but gentle and kind. 'Now the reason I have asked you all here,' he continued, 'is that I wanted to talk with you about the next stage of the Jacey Challenge.

'Just to remind you: this is *not* a competition of one person or group against another, and so there will be no winners as such. The Challenge is *from* yourself *to* yourself. And you, yourselves, will award your own marks for each stage. However, these marks are for your own satisfaction so that you can measure your own progress, and *not* to see who can be better than whom.

'To make this much more of a challenge, *all* of what you do over the period of the Challenge will become part of your final marks. Again, it will be up to yourselves to decide what marks to take away for things you feel were not so good, or for things you wish you had not done . . .'

Hattie tried to concentrate on what he was saying, but found it impossible. 'Were there more people as big as him? Had he been this big on Earth? Had he ever lived on Earth – or had he always lived in heaven? He was just like a film star.' The thoughts and questions chased themselves in quick succession through her mind. And was it her imagination, or did the ground really shake as he walked around?

Roulus continued talking for a few minutes

more, patiently and carefully answered the many questions, and then asked several of the cherubs to hand out the leaflet he had prepared.

A buzz of excitement filled the air as ideas were shared.

'Got it! Bet I know what *your* personal challenge should be,' said Jacko to Wideshoes – 'bein' best mates with Goodie!'

'Huh!' said Wideshoes. 'Roulus said it should be a challenge, not a miracle!'

'I have a nasty feeling,' said Roulus to Sacc as all the cherubs left the Great Space laughing, chattering and planning, 'that they didn't hear the bit about it not being a competition between each other, but only a challenge to themselves.'

Sacc smiled. 'Children are naturally competitive,' she replied, 'so it's to be expected really at first. They'll learn eventually that there is a better way. After all, that is part of the point of the Jacey Challenge, isn't it?'

'I do hope you are right,' Roulus said with a slight frown. Then he nodded and smiled back. 'Yes. I'm sure you are.'

CHAPTER 4

Flying Lessons and Birthday Parties

'See ya!' called Wideshoes, as Wishbone, Jacko, Tictoc and Speck wandered off to inspect Jacko's latest collection. He was an avid collector of all sorts of weird and wonderful things. Each week seemed to bring a new interest and array of items.

'And don't be late!' she added.

'O.K., O.K! Bossy Boots!' Wishbone called back, his grin softening his words.

'I'm not bossy!' replied Wideshoes indignantly.

'Are so!' Wishbone's voice came back more faintly as he ran to catch up with the others.

'Late for what?' asked Hattie curiously.

'Oh – nothing,' said Wideshoes vaguely.

'My back's really itching!' said Hattie wriggling, her curiosity distracted by the strange sensation.

'Turn round,' ordered Wideshoes. 'Hmmm. Thought so. It's your wings. They've started growing.'

'My wings?!' Hattie twisted and turned, trying in vain to see behind herself. 'What do they look like? Will I be able to use them to – to – *fly?*'

''course! How else d'y'think you'll get around? You can't use the Celecopters all the time.'

'*Awesome!*' said Hattie excitedly. 'When will they be ready?'

'Not sure,' said Wideshoes. 'You'll need lessons at the Flying School first, anyway. Everyone does who's new.'

'Couldn't you show me? Oh, go on! Please!'

Wideshoes struggled between the small inside voice that told her that she would probably get into trouble if she did, and not wanting to disappoint her new friend. 'We-e-ell. I s'pose. Well . . . O.K.' she said reluctantly.

After some searching, they found a piece of cloud that had a number of ridges of different heights. Wideshoes made Hattie do some flapping exercises, until she was satisfied that Hattie knew how to use her wings.

'Now, watch me,' she instructed. She walked to the edge of a small ridge, and jumped. Hattie watched closely as Wideshoes stepped out into space, and began to rhythmically move the small wings that grew out of her back, just below her shoulder-blades. Wideshoes glided to a halt below. She looked up at Hattie. 'Now *you* try it,' she called.

Hattie stood at the edge of the ridge. She looked down, and gulped. It had looked so easy when Wideshoes had done it, but she was not so confident now it was her turn. She felt just like she had before first jumping off the diving board when she was little. She flexed her wings. They did feel very strange: not part of her at all. What if they fell off when she tried using them? She gulped again.

'Com'n,' called Wideshoes encouragingly. 'You'll be fine. You'll see! Just jump 'n' flap.'

Hattie took a deep breath, closed her eyes, and jumped. She felt herself falling, falling, falling.

'*Flap!!*' shrieked Wideshoes.

Hattie flapped frantically. First, she zoomed to the left, then she zoomed to the right, then she zoomed to the left again. It seemed impossible to make her wings work together. Now she was going up, not down. Was she *ever* going to land?

'Help!' she screamed.

'Flap slower!' shrieked Wideshoes again.

Hattie tried to do as she was told. Now she was dropping down and down and down.

'*Help!*' she screamed again, as she crash-landed on top of Wideshoes.

The two girls lay breathless and panting for a few moments. Then Wideshoes stood up, gingerly rubbing her knee, then her elbow, then her head.

'Ouch! You weigh a *ton*!' she grumbled. Then she looked anxiously at Hattie. 'You O.K.?'

Hattie lay on her back, a rapturous look on

her face. 'I did it!' she said. 'Shall I try again? I know I'd be ever so good next time.'

'No!' said Wideshoes hurriedly. She had a nasty feeling that she was going to get into trouble for trying to teach Hattie herself. 'Are you really *reeeelly* O.K.?'

''course! Ouch!' One of Hattie's wings hung at a slightly mournful angle. The other also looked the worse for wear.

Wideshoes sighed. She had just *known*, when she had got up this morning, that this was not going to be her day. 'C'mon,' she said. 'I s'pose we'd better get someone to look at you.'

At that moment, a very well-known but very unwelcome voice from above said, 'Oh dear, Wideshoes. In trouble again? What *is* Sacc going to say?'

Wideshoes looked up. Goodie stood where Hattie had so recently launched herself for her maiden flight. Goodie smiled her superior smile, then walked away with her friend following.

Wideshoes glared after her. 'Huh! That Goodie is so – so – so *goody-goody*!'

A little later, Hattie and Wideshoes were just coming out of the General Care Centre as Sacc was going in. Wideshoes gave a halting explanation in response to Sacc's query as to why they were there.

'Oh, Wideshoes,' she sighed. 'Fancy trying to teach Sarah to fly yourself. You know the rules. She could have been really hurt. That's why we have a Flying School.'

'Yes. Sorry,' said Wideshoes despondently.

'I'm called Hattie now,' said Hattie. 'And it was my fault. I went on 'n' on at Wideshoes till she said yes. Don't be cross with her. *Please.*'

'Well,' smiled Sacc, 'so long as you're alright. That's what really matters. But you *must* remember the rules, Wideshoes. They are there for everyone's safety. Now, run along and get ready, otherwise you'll be late.'

'Late for what? What's happening?' asked Hattie, as they left.

'Oh, you know what grown-ups are like – always saying weird things,' said Wideshoes dismissively. 'C'mon!'

After a few minutes, they arrived at a delicate-looking construction made of what looked like smoky non-transparent glass.

It was cool and quiet inside and, like all the other buildings Hattie had seen since her arrival, it wasn't like anything she had been used to on Earth. It gave you the feeling you were in a kind of glass-house. From the inside you could see all that was happening outside – the surroundings, the view, everything – just as if there were no walls at all separating you from everything else. And yet, as Hattie had just realised, you could not see in from the outside.

Hattie followed Wideshoes into a very small but very pretty room with gossamer light curtains blowing gently in the breeze. Around the perimeter was all that anyone would need to store their things.

'Your room,' Wideshoes said, waving her hand around. 'Mine's next door.'

A bed with a bright spread looked soft and inviting, and Hattie gazed longingly at it. Through an open door, she could see a tiny bathroom. Wideshoes led the way in, and pressed a button. From the centre of a base which curved upwards towards the edges rose a fountain of water.

Wideshoes showed her a few more things, before saying, 'O.K.? I'm off. Gotta get cleaned up for supper. See y'.' She did a head-over-heels across Hattie's bed, then disappeared through the door.

Hattie pulled off her clothes, and stepped under the fountain. The water was lovely: just the right temperature. She closed her eyes, squished the cascading drops of water back and forth with her hand, and thought of all that had happened since she had arrived. This morning she had been in what seemed now another life, she mused dreamily. Then she opened her eyes sharply. It *was* another life! Another place that was full of all the things that had been so familiar to her up till now.

She thought of her mum and her dad, and of how much they must be missing her. Some tears rolled down her cheeks, and joined the fountain drops, as she imagined their sadness. Then a warm glow spread through her, as she remembered all their tender care through her long illness. Of how much they had always loved her, all through her life. Of how much she loved them. That would always be so, Hattie was quite sure of that.

Some more tears rolled down her cheeks, but they were for her parents, her family, her friends left behind on Earth and not for herself. She did so wish they could see her now – no longer suffering, and limited by her illness.

They – everyone she'd loved during her life on Earth – would always be so important to her. They would always be in her memory, and in her heart.

She ached to be able to tell them she was so, so happy. And that – for some strange, deeply mysterious, heavenly reason she didn't understand – she did not miss them too desperately much; and so they were not to worry about whether she was lonely or sad.

'Oh, Mum, Dad,' she whispered. 'I love you! And I do wish, I *wish* you could meet Wideshoes – and Wishbone and Speck and Tictoc – they are my new friends. There's so much I want to tell you about all that's happened.'

She said a little prayer for them as she towelled herself dry with the big fluffy towel that hung on the rail, then sprinkled herself liberally with the powder on the shelf. She wished she had some clean clothes to put on; her other ones were a bit scruffy now after all that she and the others had been doing. Hattie wandered back into the bedroom, then stopped in surprise. On the bed lay the prettiest dress. And the perfect shoes to wear with it.

She had just finished getting dressed when Wideshoes appeared at the door. Gone was her previous outfit and, in its place, she was wearing a long skirt from under which her beloved boots peeked, and a fashionable top. She had obviously been struggling to bring the wild curls under some sort of control and her halo, to which she had also obviously been giving some attention, was sparkling. She held her right hand behind her back and gestured towards Hattie with the other. 'You look ace! C'm'n.'

'Where're we going?' asked Hattie, following Wideshoes, who kept on changing the position of her right hand to keep it away from Hattie's gaze. 'What are you hiding?'

'You'll see,' came the sung reply to both questions.

Very soon, they arrived at the edge of a large open space surrounded by those mysterious telinths. Myriads of tiny twinkling lights sparkled from every bough. Coloured ribbons and streamers hung in their hundreds, fluttering and dancing in the breeze. People of all ages and nationalities were gathered there, talking and laughing. When they saw Hattie, they turned towards her.

Hattie stood still in amazement, and looked around her as everyone clapped and cheered. Wideshoes gave Hattie a hug. 'Happy Birthday, Hattie,' she said shyly, holding out a present wrapped in shiny paper and with a lopsided bow on one end. She took Hattie's hand and led her toward the crowd of people gathered who were still smiling and clapping, and who parted to disclose a huge table laden with every sort of delicious food, many of them Hattie's

favourites. In the centre was an enormous iced cake, with candles and sparklers. Another table nearby was piled high with brightly wrapped presents. Music played in the background, and Hattie recognised the tune.

Overhead, a huge banner was stretched.

HAPPY BIRTHDAY, HATTIE!

it proclaimed.
And so it was that there was a great celebration in heaven the day that Hattie arrived.

CHAPTER 5

'A Trip to Earth!'

The next day the sun shone down, warming both water and bathers alike.

Wishbone tobogganed head-first down the small waterfall on his stomach, and splashed into the pool below where many other cherubs were noisily jumping and swimming and playing around. The air buzzed with much chatter, and the main topic of discussion was the Jacey Challenge.

Tictoc sat on the bank trying to calculate how much water was going over the waterfall per second, in between joining in Wideshoes' and Hattie's conversation. They sat either side of him, also dangling their feet in the water, and talking about the Challenge. As they chatted, they were eating giant ice-flooms and did not notice Speck creeping up behind them with a bucket.

The resulting cascade of water made Wideshoes drop her ice-floom. 'Speck!' she shrieked, then picked up its remnants and chased the fleeing cherub.

When she judged she was near enough, she drew back her arm and threw the ice-floom. Not for nothing had she been practising for the Cherubs Crantball Team. Straight and true it flew. At the last second some instinct made Speck turn and, seeing the missile, he ducked.

Over his head, Wideshoes saw a figure emerge from round the corner of a rock.

'SPLAT!' The cone and its contents landed squarely in Sacc's middle. Liquorice, chocolate, orange and lime ice-floom trickled slowly down as she watched in disbelief, and Wideshoes watched in utter dismay. Reluctantly, she walked towards Sacc, dragging her feet and trying to delay the moment of reckoning as long as possible.

'Wideshoes!' sighed Sacc.

'I'm ever so, truly, terribly, most awfully sorry,' Wideshoes apologised in an anguished tone, jigging from one foot to the other. 'It was meant to hit Speck, not you.'

'Only you,' observed Sacc, 'only you, dear Wideshoes, could think of eating such a totally dreadful mixture of flavours as orange, liquorice, chocolate and lime.'

Wideshoes produced a hankie, tentatively

walked up to Sacc and began rubbing at the mess, but only succeeded in making it more widespread.

'Thank you – but no, thank you, Wideshoes,' said Sacc hurriedly. 'I'll deal with it myself. I think you had better concentrate on cleaning yourself up.' She turned away, and then turned back. 'Oh, yes. I almost forgot. After that, I'd like to see you, please.'

'I wonder what I've done *now*?' sighed Wideshoes, as she watched Sacc soar gracefully away.

Goodie had seen it all from where she had been sitting on a raised area by the waterfall. She turned and looked triumphantly at her friends who sat in a semicircle around her, and they all giggled.

A little later, Sacc looked at the cherub sitting cross-legged in the big armchair, with her hastily brushed mop of amazing brown curls that always insisted on springing up in defiance of any attempt to smooth them down. Sacc wondered, as she often did, how Wideshoes' halo managed to stay on at the precarious angle that she liked to wear it.

She thought, too, of the Conference of Angels

in Charge of Cherubs that had been held only that morning. When the subject had come around to Wideshoes, there had been quite a long conversation. 'We all love Wideshoes dearly,' everyone had agreed, there was no question about that; however, she did have the most extraordinary ability to create havoc wherever she went.

'Perhaps we should give her more responsibility,' someone had suggested at last.

'*More* responsibility?' another had said, horrified. 'Is that wise? Wouldn't that only cause *more* disasters?'

Sacc had agreed with the first speaker. 'She has been very good at making Hattie feel welcome, and at home. I think you may be right. Perhaps we need to give her the opportunity to channel her energy into a different direction.'

'She certainly has plenty of energy to channel,' the second speaker had said.

After some more conversation, they were all agreed as to what should happen.

Now Sacc felt Wideshoes' large, sea-green eyes regarding her solemnly, and she smiled. 'You and Hattie seem to be very good friends. You have made her feel very welcome. Thank you.

'We – that is, the other Senior Angels and I – were wondering if you would be prepared to do something else for us. This task would be a bit more difficult. However, I am sure that you will manage it very well.' Sacc had to resist the temptation to cross her fingers under her desk.

Wideshoes sat up a bit straighter, folded her arms in what she hoped looked a tidy and efficient way, and composed her face into an expression of polite interest.

'It would mean a trip to Earth,' continued Sacc, 'and you could consider it as your Personal Challenge for the Jacey Challenge.'

'A trip to Earth!' Wideshoes could scarcely believe her ears. The others would be so envious! You usually had to be heaps older to get to go on one of those.

She tried very hard not to drift off into a daydream, and to concentrate on what Sacc was saying. But not all the words stuck, and she left Sacc's office some time later with a lot of gaps in between the words that she remembered.

'A girl called Helen . . . hospital . . . had an accident . . . ever so sad, and not interested in anything any more . . . my task to – er – what was it . . . ?' muttered Wideshoes to herself, as she walked away kicking a pebble. What else had Sacc said?

She hummed to herself, 'I've got things to do. Places to go. People to see . . .'

'. . . and so, I've got to help her,' concluded Wideshoes importantly. She was sitting with her gang in their secret hideout. As she talked, she and Wishbone were playing a game of Frisbee with their haloes, throwing them to one another across the room.

'How?' asked Speck frowning.

'Well, I – well – you know . . .'

'No,' said Speck, 'I 'spect you don't neither.'

'I do, so. It's private. I'm not allowed to tell.' Wideshoes racked her brain. She knew she should have listened closer to Sacc, but her mind had kept wandering.

'A trip to Earth,' said Wishbone enviously. 'You're so lucky! I wonder why they picked *you* – you're a d'saster area; everyone says. I'd betta' come along 'n' look after you.'

Wideshoes picked up a cushion and threw it at him, 'I don't need looking after, thank you.' Wishbone threw it back, and then other cushions began to fly around the room as everyone joined in.

Speck thumped one against Tictoc so hard that it split. Tictoc returned the thump and that cushion split as well. The soft stuffing spilled out and began floating everywhere, before landing on every available surface – including the cherubs.

'Yuk!' said Wishbone, spitting some out of his mouth. 'Ha! You look just like a snowman, Tictoc – a *stoopid* snowman.' Tictoc took a swipe at Wishbone with another cushion and that split, too; this time it was Wishbone who was covered with cushion innards.

It was some time before order, if not tidiness, was restored. Tictoc began to click his tongue rhythmically against the roof of his mouth.

'No, Tictoc!' pleaded Wideshoes. 'Not one of your weird ideas. Not now. Please! I want things to go right f'r a change.'

Tictoc looked wounded. 'My ideas aren't weird,' he said loftily, running his fingers through his hair which was still full of cushion innards. 'Actually, *actually*, I was going to say let's talk about the Jacey Challenge. None of us has fixed on anything yet, except you.'

'I don't really understand about the Challenge,' said Hattie. 'What is it?'

'Well,' said Tictoc. 'We're all supposed to do it. I guess that'll mean you, as well. It's to help each of us to . . . hang on a sec . . .' He pulled a screwed-up copy of the leaflet Roulus had given out the day before out of his pocket, smoothed it out, and read, '"It's supposed to be fun, as well as helping each of you to learn a little more about yourself – your own weaknesses and strengths." Um . . .'

Wideshoes and Wishbone looked over his shoulder at the wrinkled bit of paper. 'There are to be three sections: Personal Challenge – Community Challenge – Group Challenge,' read Wishbone, in a very passable imitation of Roulus's voice.

Wideshoes giggled. '"The Personal Challenge: – Think of something you can do that will help you become more complete as a person. It may be about overcoming some dislike or fear,"' she continued, also in a Roulus-type voice.

'My imitation's better'n yours,' said Wishbone.

'No it's not!' replied Wideshoes heatedly.

'Yes it is,' said Speck. 'Much better.'

'Huh!' said Wideshoes, wrinkling her nose at Speck.

'"Or it may be finding out and learning about something that will make you understand yourself a bit better,"' they all continued to read in unison, before collapsing on the floor with laughter.

Tictoc grinned. 'You're just *so* childish,' he said, turning the paper so that they couldn't see it any more. 'Actually, Hattie, Roulus says here that those are just two examples of possibilities. Wideshoes is fixed up, but the rest of us haven't got anything sorted yet.'

So the conversation continued about that, and further talk of Wideshoes' visit to Earth was left for later. Soon they were deep in discussing, suggesting and planning, and sheet after sheet of paper was covered with their thoughts and ideas.

'I wonder what Goodie's lot will do,' said Wideshoes. 'We've just got to beat them.'

Tictoc sighed patiently. 'Actually, it doesn't matter, does it?' he asked. 'Remember what Roulus said? It's not supposed to be a competition. It's supposed to be a challenge to ourselves.' Tictoc was so laidback he was almost horizontal, and he just could never understand why Wideshoes spent so much time and energy on competing with Goodie. There were much more important things to be thinking about. Like scientific experiments, for instance.

'Yes. Well. Maybe,' muttered Wideshoes. Deep down, she knew Tictoc was right. 'But Goodie is such a pain . . .'

'Why don't you like Goodie?' Hattie enquired, with a puzzled frown. 'She looks really nice.'

'Huh! Don't let looks deceive you,' said Wideshoes darkly.

'But why . . . ?'

'Actually, *actually*, I don't think Wideshoes can even remember why,' said Tictoc in a bored voice and running his fingers through his hair to try to get out some of the cushion stuffing.

'I 'spect it's 'cos she's painful,' volunteered Speck.

'You mean she's a pain,' grinned Tictoc, 'not she's "painful"!'

'I'm *not* a pain,' said Wideshoes indignantly.

'Not you. Her, stoopid,' said Wishbone.

'I'm not stupid!'

Hattie sighed. It didn't look as if she was going to get an answer to her question – not today, anyway.

CHAPTER 6

Saints, Lions, Lambs and Flying Cushions

Some time later, the Gang emerged from the secret passageway with Tictoc leading and Hattie behind him. Over his shoulder she could see, some fifty metres distant, a man carrying a small lamb.

'Aahh! How cute!' thought Hattie, head on one side and smiling at the sight of the little animal. Then her smile froze in horror. Stalking the man and the lamb was absolutely the hugest lion she had ever seen.

It was massive. And yet it was obviously padding along so silently that the man seemed totally unaware of its threatening presence so close behind him. Hattie clutched at Tictoc's arm. A scream built up in her throat, but no sound would come out. Tictoc looked at her horrified expression and saucer-round eyes in puzzlement.

'What?' he asked, looking round to where she was pointing with a shaking hand and finger.

Speck, meanwhile, had wriggled his way out

to the front. Then he, too, saw the terrible danger. Immediately he was off, running as fast as he could, oblivious of his own safety and shouting at the top of his voice, '*Zanton! Zanton!*

The man and the lion turned at the same time at the sound of Speck's voice.

The lion tossed his massive head and mane, and let out a roar that echoed and re-echoed into the distance. The soundwaves, like the ripples on a pool, moved further and further outwards, bounced off distant clouds then returned as shadows of their former selves to haunt the listeners' ears. The noise was terrifying!

Boy and lion leapt at each other, and then Speck was on the ground with one of the lion's paws on top of him. The mighty mouth moved down towards the helpless boy.

'Zanton! Zanton!' the man also called, but with no sense of urgency at all it seemed. 'Stop it! Let Speck up before you lick him completely away.'

The lion obliged. Speck jumped to his feet and flung his arms around the lion's neck. A gentle rumble, a very distant cousin of that first roar, issued from the back of his throat almost like a purr.

When the man reached them he placed the lamb gently on the ground, and Speck transferred his hug to him. The man returned the hug enthusiastically, twirled him round, then set him on the back of the lion. Speck's hands and forearms disappeared into the great mane, as his fingers scrabbled for a hold. He was laughing with delight, as was the man.

Hattie stood dumbfounded, and rubbed her eyes: she must be dreaming. Around her, the others were exclaiming,

'It's St. Francis!'

'Hi, Francis!'

'Ooh, Francis – can *I* have a ride, too?'

Hattie followed them as they gathered round the man, who ruffled the hair of one, put his arm around another, and winked at the third. 'Hello, Hattie,' he smiled.

'You know my name?' she asked, amazed.

'Of course.' He smiled his gentle smile again. For the first time, Hattie noticed the many-coloured and different-sized butterflies and birds fluttering around his head. The birdsong carolled their contentment at being in Francis' presence. A fledgling nestled in his cupped hand.

The lamb, meanwhile, had trotted over to

the lion who carefully, so as not to unseat Speck, bent his legs until his belly was resting on the ground. The lamb settled itself comfortably between the lion's front paws, and Speck leaned forwards until his cheek was lying against the great shaggy mane. There the three of them remained, quite still and obviously totally content in one another's company.

Francis' eyes followed Hattie's gaze as she watched all this.

'That'd never've happened on Earth,' she said wonderingly.

'Not yet. But, one day . . .' replied Francis.

The fledgling in his hand chirruped as if to remind Francis of his needs and, at once, his whole attention focused on to the bird. 'Look. See?' he said. 'She's broken her leg.' The children watched fascinated as he tenderly and skilfully put on a tiny splint.

Meanwhile, he reminded them of how important it was to take care of every part of God's creation, whatever or whoever it was, but especially the small and the vulnerable; and he entertained them with stories of some of his many encounters with the animals and birds that had been so much a part of his life on Earth.

The next night, Hattie and Wideshoes curled up on Hattie's bed before going to sleep, talking about Wideshoes' Earth visit the next day.

They lay on their stomachs, chins cupped on hands, looking out at an enormous round orange-coloured moon set upon a velvet-black sky. Stars, near and far, twinkled and shimmered. A sweetbird's song confidently broke the dark stillness, its clear and delicate notes ringing like invisible bells through the night air. Nearby, other sweetbirds sang back in response. Hattie had never heard birdsong like it before.

'Don't they sound *beautiful?*' she said wonderingly.

They listened for a while, the sound sending tingles through them.

'You nervous?' Hattie asked after another pause.

'No – well – yes – I guess . . . But Sacc said that she'll be keepin' an eye on ev'rything, so I shan't really be on my own. She said, "I'd never send anyone on their own until I was certain they know what they're doing, and can handle whatever comes up,"' quoted Wideshoes, doing a very passable imitation of Sacc's voice.

Hattie giggled appreciatively. 'You're better at doing Sacc than Roulus. Anyway, you'll be great,' she added loyally. 'You'll see.'

That night, Wideshoes dreamt that she, Hattie, Speck and Wishbone were floating lazily through the sky on cushions.

All of a sudden, Tictoc roared by. 'I've invented a motor-cushion!' he yelled. 'And it really works! Look, I can actually loop the loop!' Over and over he went, until the others were so dizzy with watching him that they felt they, too, were spinning round and round and round . . .

CHAPTER 7

'Who on Earth . . . ?!'

Wideshoes turned over and over in bed, finally landing on the floor in a tangle of bedding. She opened her eyes, and then remembered her dream. 'Trust Tictoc t' wake me up,' she sighed.

The early morning sun slanted through her window. 'Today was to be special . . . What was it?' Wideshoes rubbed her eyes and yawned sleepily, as her memory slowly got into gear. Then she sat bolt upright, suddenly wide awake. Today she was going to Earth!! She disentangled herself and rushed around getting ready.

Before long, Wideshoes stood with Sacc at the foot of a bed. Its occupant, a girl of about Wideshoes' age, was fast asleep.

'Now, remember what I told you,' said Sacc softly. 'You know what to do if you need me.' Then she disappeared from view.

The butterflies inside Wideshoes' stomach fluttered round once more, and then also disappeared. She tiptoed to the other end of the bed, and looked down at the girl. Damp eyelashes lay against flushed cheeks.

'She's b'n crying,' thought Wideshoes. 'That's so sad.'

The girl was restless and suddenly turned over, flinging one arm out as she did so.

Wideshoes stepped back quickly to get out of the way, and stubbed her toe on the nearby locker. 'Ouch!' she muttered. She hopped around on the other leg whilst hanging on to her sore foot. A hop or two later she caught the other foot in the trailing bedding and toppled over, pulling it off the bed as she did so. For the second time that morning she was tangled up in sheet and duvet.

The girl in the bed woke up. In the dim light she saw a pair of large, sea-green eyes looking at her from the midst of her bedding. 'Who are *you*?' she gasped, opening her mouth wider as if to scream.

'No! Don't!' said Wideshoes hurriedly. 'I'm here to help you. Really, *reeelly*. Honest!'

Mouth still open, the girl regarded her suspiciously.

'My name is Wideshoes. I'm an angel. Well, a cherub,' Wideshoes rushed on. 'I've been sent here to help you. And your name's Helen.'

'How do you know that?' Helen was still

suspicious. 'If you're really an angel, how come I can see you? Angels live in heaven. Have I died'n gone to heaven?'

'Nope. Sorry. You're still on Earth. In hospital.' Wideshoes' irrepressible grin dimpled her cheeks.

'Don't want your help, anyway. Don't want nobody's help!' Helen threw herself back down on the pillow, and squeezed her eyes tight shut. 'Go away, else I'll scream! Bet you're not an angel, anyway. Who believes in angels?!'

'I am! I am!' said Wideshoes desperately. 'Look, Helen. Please look. Please let me show you. Then, if you still don't believe me, I'll go. Honest I will.'

Helen opened her eyes a little, and watched Wideshoes suspiciously.

'You can see me 'cause I let you. Watch!' Wideshoes concentrated. 'Bet y'can't see me now, can you?'

'Ooh! It's weird. I can still see your right hand, your left ear, and your feet. But the rest of you's gone,' said Helen, raising herself up on one arm.

'Bother!' said Wideshoes crossly, reappearing. 'I'll have to practise that a bit more. You believe me now, though?'

'Yes. No. I – I s'pose.' Helen seemed to lose

interest in the conversation, turned her back on Wideshoes, and pulled the covers that Wideshoes had piled back onto the bed over her ears.

Wideshoes looked at the back of Helen's head, and chewed her lip uncertainly.

'Helen,' she began tentatively.

There was a muffled 'Mmmm?'

'Please tell me what's wrong.'

'Everything.'

'What's ev'rything?'

'Nothing.'

Wideshoes could tell this was not going to be a very fruitful conversation, so she changed tack. 'Bye, then,' she said.

It worked. Helen turned over and looked warily over the top of the bedding. 'Don't go.'

'O.K. I'll stay – but only if you tell me what's wrong.'

Helen paused, took a deep breath as if about to speak, let it out again as if she had changed her mind, drew in another, then began to speak; jerkily at first, but with gathering speed as her story unfolded.

'I'm here 'cos I had an accident. The doctors said I won't be able to walk again, and – and – and – that I'll have to use that horrid thing

there for ever 'n' ever!' she finished in a rush.
She gestured towards a wheelchair that was
folded in the corner. 'I hate it. I hate it! I'd
rather die. I wanted to be a dancer when I was
older. It's so – so – so unfair!' Tears began to
roll down her cheeks.

They also began to run down Wideshoes face,
as she listened. 'That's really *reeelly* awful,' she
agreed sympathetically. There was a pause, and
she wiped her face with her hand. 'What's it
like? You know. Using a wheelchair.'

'Don't know. Don't care. The doctors and
nurses and Mum and Dad – and everyone – keep
on 'n' on at me to have a go. But I won't. I won't!'

'Why not?'

'Because . . . because . . . 'cause if I do that's
like me saying I know what they say's true, and
that I won't probably walk again – let alone
dance!' More tears began to fall.

'C'n I have a go?'

Helen shrugged disinterestedly. 'If you like.
I don't care.'

Wideshoes struggled to open the chair,
caught her finger and, in waving it around,
knocked her arm against the jug and glass on
the locker. Over they went with a crash.

A moment later, the door opened, and a nurse looked in. 'Are you alright, Helen dear?' she asked, then saw the jug and glass on the floor. 'Oh dear. I'll just clear that up, and then you can go back to sleep.'

Wideshoes meanwhile, not having had enough time to make herself invisible, dived under the bed and into a puddle of water from the jug. 'Oh, yuk!' she hissed.

'What did you say, dear?' asked the nurse.

'Oh. Oh, nothing. Just – just – sorry,' stuttered Helen.

'Not to worry,' smiled the nurse, patting her arm. 'You just go back to sleep. Is there anything you want? A nice warm drink? No? Alright. Nunight.'

She left the room, softly closing the door, and Wideshoes clambered out. Helen started to giggle at Wideshoes forlorn expression and appearance.

'Huh!' said Wideshoes, then began to giggle as well. Soon there were more tears running down their faces, but this time they were tears of laughter and not of sadness.

'Tell you what,' said Wideshoes when she had finally managed to open the wheelchair, and had sat herself in it, 'this is ace. You should try it.' She gave a few tentative pushes with her feet and began to propel herself around the room. Moments later, she collided with the locker. Once again, over went the newly filled jug and, once again, Wideshoes had to dive under the bed as the nurse entered.

'Helen, dear,' she said in a concerned voice. 'What's wrong? Were you having a nightmare?'

'Er – no. That is, yes. Yes, I was. Sorry.'

'That's alright, dear. It's not your fault.' The nurse cleared up the spilled water and filled up the jug from the washbasin. Helen held her breath in case she noticed the wheelchair was open. Fortunately, she didn't in the dim light. 'Do you want me to sit with you for a while?'

'Oh! No. No! Thank you. I'll be fine now. Honest.'

'Well. If you're sure. If you need me, just ring the buzzer.' The nurse once again left the room, and closed the door gently behind her.

Wideshoes crawled out once more. 'I'm soaked,' she said mournfully, holding out her arms to emphasise what she was saying. Once more, they collapsed into giggles.

'Put my dressing gown on,' said Helen when she could get enough breath to speak. 'And put your clothes on the radiator to dry.'

Cosy and warm, Wideshoes curled up at the end of Helen's bed and propped her head on her hand. 'Why're you in here – and not in that big room with all the others?'

'They're all babies!' said Helen scornfully. 'There's nobody my age. I was so mis'r'ble in there with them all squawking and gurgling, that the doctor said I should have my own room, so's I can do what I want when I want.'

'Aren't you lonely?'

'No. Yes. Don't care if I am. Don't care about anything.'

'Helen,' Wideshoes said after a while. 'Let me take you out in your wheelchair later?'

'No! I'm never, ever, going out in that thing.'

Wideshoes got off the bed, took off the dressing gown, and began to pull on her clothes.

'What are you doing? Where're you going?' asked Helen in a dismayed tone.

'Well, I'm not allowed to stay if you won't let me help you.'

'But – but . . .'

'Bye,' said Wideshoes.

'If I say – if I say yes, will you stay then?'

'Yup!' said Wideshoes, pulling off her damp t-shirt in relief, pulling the dressing gown back on, and landing with a bounce on the end of the bed once more. She laid her head down on the duvet, and was asleep in a moment.

Helen watched her for a while. 'A real angel!' she thought. It was amazing. Then her eyelids began to droop and she, too, slept.

CHAPTER 8

Wishbone as Well

The slanting sun shining through the window woke Wideshoes first. She yawned and rubbed her eyes.

''otcha!' said a familiar voice, from the wheelchair.

'Wishbone!' shrieked Wideshoes. 'What in heaven are you doing here!'

'Tol' y' you needed someone t' look after you. Me f'rinstance. Sacc agreed.'

'You mean you went on 'n' on 'n' on at her till she gave in! Well, you can go right back. I don't need you here. This is *my* Challenge. Not yours. Go *away*!'

Helen woke at that moment, yawned, then saw Wishbone in the wheelchair. 'Who's he?' she asked, wide-eyed.

Reluctantly, Wideshoes introduced Wishbone. 'He's just going,' she said, narrowing her eyes meaningfully at him.

'Oh, *please* let him stay,' pleaded Helen, her eyes sparkling with excitement at the visit of not just one, but two, angels. 'It's a pity,' she thought, 'that no one will believe me when I tell them.'

The door opened, and the nurse stood at the threshold in surprise. 'This is a bit early for visitors, Helen,' she said disapprovingly.

'Oh, please let them stay! They're my special friends. They – they want to take me out in my wheelchair later – just around outside. In the hospital garden, that is. Can they? Please?'

The nurse looked astonished, then she smiled brightly at Wishbone and Wideshoes. 'That's wonderful! Of course they can stay, as long as they like. Have you had breakfast yet, children?'

'No, they haven't. And I want cereal, bacon buttie, toast, peanut butter and blackcurrant jam, juice an' – an' – and I think that's all. Please? And can they have the same?'

The nurse's eyes had widened, and her jaw dropped, as Helen proceeded through the menu. 'Good heavens! I don't think you've eaten that much altogether since you came into hospital. This is really amazing. I hope you two don't have to rush off. You're obviously a marvellous influence on her.'

A few minutes later, a trolley was wheeled in

with the banquet that Helen had asked for, and the children tucked in.

'I'm stacked,' sighed Wishbone contentedly, settling back in the wheelchair. 'A bit 'a shut-eye now, I think.'

'Oh, no you don't!' said Wideshoes firmly. She tipped the chair so that he tumbled out. 'You wanted to stay. So, you can do something useful. Like dis'pear whilst I help Helen get dressed. And whilst you're dis'pearing . . . pr'aps you'd make it perm'nent?'

Oh, no!' said Helen. 'I want him to stay.'

Wishbone grinned triumphantly at Wideshoes, who wrinkled her nose at him, and sighed.

After some encouragement, the two cherubs persuaded Helen to sit in the wheelchair. They held the chair steady whilst Helen slid herself onto it from the bed, in the way she had been taught by the hospital staff. 'See?' said Wideshoes, as she fastened the safety belt across Helen's middle, 'It's not so bad, is it?'

Helen shrugged, and didn't reply. After a while, she pushed herself over to the TV. Wideshoes did a thumbs-up sign to Wishbone, and grinned delightedly.

'Look,' said Helen, putting a video into the

player, and turning on the TV. 'This is the dance project my mum wants me to do. She gave me this video to encourage me to say yes. It's for disabled kids like – like – me. And for able-bodied kids. Dancing together. I think it's stupid!'

The three of them sat and watched in silence for a while.

'Oh – I dunno,' said Wishbone. 'I wouldn' mind 'avin' a go.' He stood on a low horizontal bar at the side of the chair, held onto the back with one hand, threw the other arm into the air with his hand bent into what he hoped looked an artistic pose, and dropped his head back.

Wideshoes stood on the opposite side, and mimicked his pose. 'Go on, Helen,' she urged. 'Put your hands above your head in an arch – that's it! Go on. Higher! I bet we look ace!' She kicked one leg out dramatically, and caught her foot on the side of the bed. 'Ouch!' She hopped around, rubbing her foot for the second time that day. 'We need more space. I know. Let's go in the corridor.'

After a bit of a struggle as the chair wheels seemed to have a mind of their own, Wideshoes and Wishbone managed to maneouvre it through the door. They were so busy with the chair, they did not realise the corridor sloped gently, nor that they had neglected to put on the brake.

'Right,' said Wideshoes. 'Let's try again.' She climbed up on to the arm rests so that she was standing on them and facing Helen, then reached down and placed her hands on Helen's shoulders. Wishbone, meanwhile, did a neat handstand on the footrests and Helen reached forward, held onto his legs, and threw her head back so that she was looking up at Wideshoes.

'Bet we really look ace now,' Wishbone said, from his upside-down position.

At that moment, the chair began to move under the combined weight of the children.

'Quick! Put on the brake!' screeched down Wideshoes.

'Where is it?' Helen screeched back up at her.

'*I* dunno!'

Meanwhile, the chair gathered momentum until it seemed to be flying along. Down the corridor – which led to a delivery ramp for porters' trolleys – they sped.

From his upside-down position Wishbone, who had witnessed every hair-raising moment

of their journey, watched the doors approach ever nearer, his eyes getting wider and wider.

Crash! The wheelchair hit the big swing doors open, then careered across the courtyard outside, bumping madly over the gaps in the crazy paving.

Beyond the courtyard, a stretch of grass sloped gently up towards an ornamental pond.

The journey across the lawn slowed the

momentum of the chair, which finally jolted to a stop against the low wall surrounding the pond. Unfortunately, Wideshoes carried on.

SPLASH!

Wishbone righted himself, then doubled over in laughter at the sight of Wideshoes standing knee-deep in water, and surrounded by waterlilies on which were perched some very bewildered-looking frogs. She put her hands on her hips, and glared at Wishbone. 'Well, don't help a lady out then, will you,' she said haughtily. 'This is the third time I've got wet today!'

By now, Wishbone was lying on his back, kicking his legs in the air, and then rolling around with laughter. 'Soz!' he gasped, eventually, 'soz. But – but –'

Wishbone's laugh was so infectious, Helen began to giggle too. Wideshoes transferred her glare to her, then she also began to giggle. She waded ashore, and flopped down onto the grass next to Wishbone. After a while she sat up, took off her boots, and began emptying out the pond water. She twiddled her toes.

'Wonder if anyone saw us?' she said, looking cautiously around her as if expecting an irate army of hospital staff to jump out at them demanding what on earth they thought they were doing.

Miraculously, it seemed that no one had.

'How did you manage to hang on, Wishbone?' asked Helen admiringly. 'You were ever so clever.'

Wishbone shrugged modestly, secretly ever so pleased at Helen's praise. 'Some've us can 'old on better 'n others,' he said, looking sideways at Wideshoes – who promptly emptied the remaining water in her boots over him. 'Oh, yuk! That's 'sgusting!'

Inside the hospital, Helen's doctor paused in the course of his rounds and looked through the window at the children sunning themselves. 'It really is amazing. You're quite right; it's like a miracle. I was getting seriously worried about that child; she seemed to be slipping further and further away from us. But now look at her.'

He and the nurses with him watched as Wideshoes and Wishbone began wheeling Helen's chair round in circles, then running along in a straight line, then more circles. Finally, unaware that they were being observed, they did another impromptu dance scenario, culminating in Wishbone doing a backflip off the chair, whilst Wideshoes and Helen gracefully swayed their arms backwards and forwards.

The laughter of the three drifted in at the window. The doctor and nurses applauded their antics, and smiled at the happy sound.

'Look!' said the doctor. 'Helen's propelling her chair on her own now. Marvellous! Perhaps we can arrange a little trip into town when Helen's used to maneouvring her chair in the hospital grounds, and has increased sufficiently in confidence. At the rate she is going, though, that should only be a few days.' He turned reluctantly away from the window. 'Ah, well. Better get on with the ward round, I suppose.'

The rest of the morning passed happily, messing around in the hospital gardens. Wishbone and Wideshoes pushed Helen's chair under the enormous canopy of branches of a great weeping willow tree, then perched themselves on a low-sweeping branch beside her. There the three of them sat hidden by the foliage, talking, laughing and seeing who could tell the worst jokes. 'You're bound to win, Wishbone,' Wideshoes assured him. 'You tell the worstest jokes of anyone ever.'

Finally, hunger drove them indoors. When

food arrived, Helen again put away as much as the cherubs.

After they had eaten their fill, the three lay on the bed and stared up at the ceiling. 'This has been the best time,' sighed Helen, and yawned. She was a very different person from the one Wideshoes had first seen early that morning. Her eyes were bright, as was her voice, and there was colour in her cheeks.

'Mmmm . . . you bet,' agreed the other two, yawning as well.

A few minutes later, all three were curled up on the bed and sound asleep.

Wishbone woke first. The afternoon sun's rays slanted in the windows opposite to where the morning rays had shone in heralding the arrival of the cherub. It seemed such ages ago. He nudged Wideshoes. 'We gotta go,' he whispered.

'I want to stay,' declared Wideshoes, yawning, then settling down again. 'I want to stay with Helen.'

Wishbone continued patiently to prod her, until she was awake. 'We gotta go,' he repeated.

Wideshoes frowned. 'I s'pose . . .' she said reluctantly. They both looked at the sleeping

Helen. 'Helen,' she called softly, shaking her shoulder. 'Helen. Wake up.'

Helen yawned, stretched and sat up. 'What's wrong?' she asked, seeing the cherubs' troubled expressions.

'We've got to go – I'm really *reeelly* sorry,' said Wideshoes, a mournful look on her face.

'Please, please stay,' begged Helen, clasping Wideshoes' hand, and looking from one to the other. 'Don't go!'

'You'll be fine now. You'll see,' said Wideshoes, reluctantly taking her hand from Helen's. She reached over and gave her a hug. 'Look after yourself. That disabled 'n' able-bodied dance project thingy whatsit – you will do it, won't you? Promise?'

''course I promise.' Helen turned to Wishbone and gave him a hug too, which he returned sheepishly. 'You will come back and see me, won't you?' she asked anxiously.

Wideshoes and Wishbone grinned, nodded – and disappeared. Helen stared longingly at the spot they had vacated.

The door opened, and one of the nurses came in. 'Did your friends have to go, Helen dear? That's a shame. Never mind. We'll look forward to seeing them again another day. Your mother and father are here. I was just telling them they are in for a lovely surprise.'

Wideshoes and Wishbone watched Helen's parents looking and listening in delighted amazement as their bright-eyed daughter chattered on excitedly. 'Oh, Mum, Dad – I've had *the* best day. You'll never believe all what's happened . . .'

The cherubs grinned and did a thumbs-up sign at each other, before joining hands and closing their eyes in order to concentrate better on the journey home.

CHAPTER 9

'Who Is Jacey?'

'Perhaps we shouldn't have sent her.'

'She's too young.'

'It was too much to expect from someone of her age.'

The Conference of Angels in Charge of Cherubs were discussing Wideshoes once more, this time with some concern because, since her return, she had not been her usual self.

'She has certainly been very quiet and serious and unsettled,' agreed Sacc. 'But I still don't feel it was a mistake to send her. I think I know who should speak to her.'

'Of course!' said everyone a few moments later, all in agreement with Sacc's suggestion.

'Come on, Wideshoes! Else we'll be ever so late for school if you don't get a move on!' called Hattie crossly, as she turned back yet again.

Wideshoes was walking slowly and reluctantly. She was dragging and scuffling her feet, and kept dropping behind her friend.

Hattie shielded her eyes against a bright

light behind Wideshoes. It was so vivid she had to close her eyes for a moment.

When she opened them again, Wideshoes had stopped, and seemed to be listening intently. Hattie could not see anything, but Wideshoes exclaimed, as if in reply to an invisible someone, 'Yes?'

Then she spun round, and began racing towards the light that now dazzled in its intensity. 'Jacey! Oh, *Jacey!*' Even from where she was, Hattie could hear the happiness in Wideshoes' voice.

Wideshoes leapt at the centre of the light and, mysteriously, remained suspended there. Meanwhile, the light seemed to twirl Wideshoes round and round, before setting her down on the ground.

All the while, Hattie could hear Wideshoes excited chatter and laughter, but could not make out what it was she was saying. Then, with one arm raised in the air as if her hand was being held, Wideshoes skipped off in the opposite direction to Hattie, with the great pillar of dazzling light beside her.

Hattie watched in horrified disbelief. 'Wideshoes, where are you going?' she cried. 'Who – who's that – that person you're going with? Don't you know you must never, ever go off with strangers? Wideshoes! Oh, Wideshoes, come back!' Hattie's voice faded to a whisper as she watched Wideshoes disappear from view. 'Who was the person she'd gone with? If you could call a pillar of light a "person". What was it she had called out as she ran towards it? Janey? Joucy? Jacey? *Jacey*! That was it!' The same name as the Challenge that was so engaging the attention and interest and efforts of all the Midi Cherubs.

Hattie rushed into her classroom. 'Something awful's happened to Wideshoes,' she sobbed. She panted out the story of what had happened. 'She kept calling it Jacey, Jacey. And her face looked all excited and smiley – not at all like she's been since she came back. It was all so *weird*.'

Her teacher smiled. 'It's alright, Hattie. There is no need to worry. I know who she is with, and she could not be in better hands. She's quite safe.'

'But . . .'

'You're right: children on Earth must never go off with strangers. But here it is different. Besides, Wideshoes knows Jacey, as she calls him. We all do. Wideshoes will be her old self when she returns.'

'But where's she gone? Will she be gone for long?' asked Hattie feeling very bewildered still. 'Who is Jacey? Is it a person?'

Again her teacher smiled. 'I'm sure Wideshoes will be able to explain everything much better than I can. She will be back when Jacey thinks she is ready. Now, go and sit down. It's time for some work.'

Hattie found it difficult to concentrate on

anything that day. Every few minutes, her eyes would stray to the great windows which stretched from floor to ceiling, and which almost made you feel you were sitting outside in the sunshine. 'What was Wideshoes doing? Where was she? Who was Jacey?' No one else seemed to be surprised by what Hattie had seen – except Hattie.

Hattie no sooner felt she was beginning to understand this heaven place, when something new and mysterious would happen, and she would realise how much there still was for her to learn. 'It's like there's this great secret which everyone else knows about except me. But, it couldn't be a secret if everyone knew about it – could it?' Hattie thought. She frowned, puzzled and bewildered. 'Heaven is certainly a place of surprises. Still, it makes for a fun and exciting place to be, with scarcely a dull moment!'

Hattie smiled to herself as she remembered some of the adventures she had had already. Only the previous evening she and Speck, and Tictoc . . . not Wideshoes, though; she had not wanted to join in, unusually for her. 'Wideshoes, where are you? What are you doing?' Hattie now murmured to herself. Then she felt Tictoc, who was sitting beside her, give her a nudge.

'Hattie!' he hissed out of the side of his mouth.

'Mmm?' said Hattie dreamily.

'Hattie!' This time it was not Tictoc's voice, but that of the teacher. Hattie dragged her gaze from the windows to the classroom. All eyes were on her, and she blushed a deep red.

'Hattie,' said her teacher, with a sigh. 'Stop worrying! I told you, Wideshoes will be fine. Now, Tictoc, will you show her where we are in the book, and perhaps you will do a bit of work, Hattie, please, instead of daydreaming.'

At last, school was over. 'Want to come and see my great new invention that I've just perfected?' asked Tictoc, as they walked out together. 'Actually, though I say it myself, it really *is* rather amazingly brilliant.'

'I suppose . . .' said Hattie unenthusiastically. 'I wanted to be around when Wideshoes got back though.'

'Oh, she'll probably be ages yet. She won't want to leave Jacey.'

'Who *is* Jacey? What's he like?'

'Jacey's – well . . . Jacey,' said Tictoc vaguely. 'He's difficult to describe. He's not like anybody else, actually.'

'He's ever so bright,' said Hattie, remembering the dazzling light.

'Oh, yes. He's really, really clever,' agreed Tictoc in an envious tone. 'Much cleverer than me. But he's got this kind of knack of making you feel you're the clever one. Actually, he's really neat. Are you coming, or aren't you?' he added, losing interest in their conversation.

On the way they met Speck, Wishbone and Jacko who decided they all wanted to see the invention as well.

Tictoc led the way to the Workshop where he spent a lot of his time. On a workbench there was a complicated structure with many wires, knobs, and buttons at various points, and Tictoc explained with pride its many uses. 'I've wired it into the Walkway energy to test it out,' he said as, with a flourish, he pushed down several switches.

There was a loud bang, and everything went dark. Wishbone and Jacko doubled up with laughter, Speck held his nose in disgust at the awful smell, and Hattie looked sympathetic.

'Oh! That's just *so* good!' gasped Jacko. 'Just wait till I tell everyone. They'll never believe your latest disaster!'

'Shut up, Jacko,' retorted Tictoc crossly. 'Actually, they don't usually go wrong. Anyway, just because you couldn't invent anything. All you can do is collect stupid bits of rubbish. What sort of pastime's that?'

'What d'you mean "rubbish"?' said Jacko indignantly, jumping to his feet. 'It's not . . .'

Roulus appeared in the doorway just then, and enquired whether Tictoc had any idea why all the lights on all the Walkways in the area had gone out. He listened gravely to Tictoc's embarrassed explanation.

'It was very irresponsible of you, Tictoc, to have tampered with the Walkway energy. You could have really hurt yourself and the others. The fact that we are now immortal does not give you permission to act in a dangerous manner, for whatever reason.'

Jacko suppressed a chortle of laughter, and Tictoc went very red. He glared at Jacko as he ran his fingers through his hair.

'Yes,' he said. 'I suppose . . . actually, yes – I should have been more responsible. I'm really very sorry.' He paused, then looked up uncertainly at Roulus. 'Er – can I actually – um – help repair the damage?'

Roulus nodded in approval. 'That sounds good to me.'

Hattie watched Roulus as he walked off, still amazed by his size. Was it her imagination, or did the ground really shake under his footsteps?

Tictoc went off to his self-imposed task, and the others 'Jumhoflied' – a complicated game which was currently a favourite with the Midi Cherubs and which was a mixture of hopping, jumping and flying, with a whole host of sub-rules – off in the opposite direction. Hattie Jumhoflied into her room.

Wideshoes was lying on Hattie's bed, with her feet up on the wall.

CHAPTER 10

Hattie Gets Her Answer

'Wideshoes!' exclaimed Hattie. 'Where've you been? You've really missed ever such a lot. Tictoc made this invention, but it blew up. And Roulus . . .'

'Hi,' said Wideshoes dreamily, tilting her head back to look at her friend.

'Hi. We've . . .'

'I've been with Jacey,' said Wideshoes, gazing up at the ceiling. 'Oh, Hattie, I've had such a lovely day.' She rolled over onto her side, and propped her head on her hand so that she could see her friend better.

Hattie curled up on the bed beside her. 'Who *is* Jacey? I kept asking 'n' asking, but nobody would give me a proper answer.'

Wideshoes looked at her incredulously. 'You don't know who Jacey is? Don't believe you! Jacey. J.C. Jesus Christ, silly!

''course I know who Jesus is,' said Hattie defensively. Then her eyes widened, 'That was – that was – HIM?'

'Yup!'

'That light was him? That was a – a person?'

'Yup!'

'But I could only see light.'

'It's diff'rent when you know what to look for,' said Wideshoes. 'You have to kind of, sort of, well, look *into* the light . . . and he's there. In the middle.'

'What did you do? Where did you go? You look different. All kind of glowy and cheery.'

'Oh, Hattie. We had such an ace time.' Wideshoes rocked backwards and forwards as she spoke. 'We walked. We talked. We talked heaps 'n' heaps. We played games. We went to this dearest little place I've never been to before, where there's a dell, and a tiny little pool which collects raindrops and is all sparkly and clear. And we sat there, and squished our feet in the water.

'Then we paddled some, and then Jacey produced food from somewhere – all my favourites. He showed me how to climb this hugely 'normous tree, and we sat all snuggly amongst the leaves right near this nest and watched the baby birds, and the mum and dad birds feeding them. Jacey spoke to them, so they weren't scared, and they didn't fly away.

'Then, *then* we went on this sort of, like, Magical Mystery Tour. We went to this beautiful, gorgeous place . . . I've never been there before, either. It was all yellows and golds and glittery. It felt kind of . . . kind of . . .' Wideshoes frowned and chewed her lip, as she struggled to find the right words. 'It felt kind of really happy. I wished I could have stayed, but Jacey said not yet, but I'd go there again one day.'

Wideshoes looked wistful and faraway, as she remembered. 'We talked about my visit to Earth, and about Helen. And he thanked me for doing so well, and said how proud he was of me and Wishbone . . . Helen's started that dance project thingummy whatsit, and is ever, ever so much better. Then he brought me back here. He gave me a great big hug, and told me how special I am, and how much he loved me, and that he wanted me to be happy again. I didn't want him to go, but he said I knew that he's always there. Close by, even if I can't see him. 'n' so he'll always be there anyway when I do want him.'

'Why just you?' asked Hattie, jealous at such special treatment.

'Not *just* me, silly. You, too. He's there for everyone who asks.' Wideshoes giggled. 'Even Tictoc and Speck and Wishbone. Now, tell me 'bout Tictoc's invention. What happened?'

Hattie recounted the events of that afternoon. Wideshoes rolled around the bed in glee, and gurgled with laughter as she listened.

Hattie lay in bed later, staring into the dark, and thinking about the day. She thought about Roulus. And about Jacey. She felt another stab of jealousy. 'Wideshoes seemed to have had such a special day. I'm glad for her – of *course* I am – but I do wish I could've been there, too.'

When she had gone to Children's Church on Earth, her teacher had said that Jesus was always with you, wherever you were. But then she'd been on Earth, and Jesus had been in heaven. Now she was in heaven where Jesus lived – so, was it different? She was sure it couldn't be; not from what she'd seen and heard up till now. Not from what Wideshoes had said earlier. But she did feel all confused. She'd have to ask someone. Sacc maybe? Or Roulus?

Hattie yawned. 'Perhaps I could pretend I

need him for a particular reason,' she thought sleepily. 'I wonder if he'd guess?' She yawned again. Her eyelids drooped shut, and she slept.

Hattie woke very early the next morning. She had this very strong urge to get up straight away, and go out for a walk. She glanced into Wideshoe's room, but she was curled up into a small ball, and was fast asleep. Hattie was glad. For some reason, she really wanted to be on her own.

She wandered along for a few minutes, before finding a path she and Wideshoes often used. After a few metres it opened out into a wide space, in the middle of which was a huge telinth. Its multicoloured leaves caught the early morning sun, the sparkling rainbow lights reflecting off in all directions, and turned the air around into a mass of glowing colours.

Seated on the ground, and leaning against the trunk, was a figure she recognised. He also seemed to be surrounded by light, and it was difficult to see where the telinth light ended and his began.

'Jacey!' she said wonderingly.

He smiled gently at her. 'Hello, Hattie,' he said. 'I've been waiting for you to come.'

His voice was like liquid fire; it seemed to flow over and through her, warming her, lighting her up, and making her feel all happy and safe. Like Roulus, he seemed as if he would have the strength of a Samson, yet also the gentleness of a lamb.

She stood still, looking at him silently. It didn't seem to matter that she could not think of anything to say – as if words weren't necessary in order for them to understand each other.

'Have you settled in well?' he asked. 'Are you happy here?'

Hattie got the definite feeling that he already knew the answers to all the questions he might ever ask – of her or of anyone – but that it was his way to let people tell their own stories in their own way.

'Oh, yes. Yes!' she replied. She sat herself down at his side and, before she knew it, she was pouring out the details of absolutely everything that she had thought, said and done since her arrival.

Jacey, meanwhile, sat with his head on one side watching the expressions playing across her face, listening intently to her every word, and completely absorbed in every detail of what she was saying.

Every so often, he encouraged her to talk further about certain things – 'The very things, thought Hattie, which are most important to me. How does he know?' Then she smiled to herself. 'Because he's Jacey, of course, silly!' When she finally stopped talking, there was a silence.

Then Jacey began to speak, and his every word held her spellbound.

He talked about everything that she had been thinking and puzzling over, and helping her to understand it all. He told her stories which were funny and sad and happy and beautiful and which, when she thought about them later, she realised were in fact all about her.

He had this mysterious way of knowing exactly how to say things so that she understood perfectly what he meant.

'I'm hungry,' he said eventually. 'I'll bet you are too.' Without waiting for her reply, he reached out, and pulled over a basket that had been lying on the ground nearby. Inside, was a wonderful picnic.

'Oohh. All my *best* things,' said Hattie wide-eyed, taking her absolute favourite from his outstretched hand. 'Thank you!'

Then it was time to go. This time it was Hattie who danced and skipped along beside the great dazzling pillar of light, her hand firmly clasped in his.

They arrived back, to find a glum Wideshoes sitting on the ground, her chin cupped in her hand. At the sight of Hattie and her companion, she jumped up and rushed over. 'Jacey! Oh, Jacey! You've met Hattie!'

'I've always known Hattie,' he smiled. He knelt down, and hugged both the cherubs. 'Now it's time for school,' he said firmly. 'Off you go now. Otherwise you'll be late. And no, Wideshoes, you can't have a day off,' he added with a laugh, anticipating her request as she drew in her breath.

He watched them go until they were out of sight. Every so often they turned round, waved and blew kisses, and each time he smiled and waved back. His love seemed to reach out and embrace them, even when he was no longer in view. And Hattie knew the answer to her questions of the night before; that she had no need to worry, and that he was always there for her, even when she could not see him.

CHAPTER 11

'It'll Be O.K. Trust Me!'

It was as though a switch had been thrown. Wideshoes' time with Jacey had transformed her. She was back to being her old self with a vengeance. Wanting to share her happy state with everyone else, she went about trying to 'Do Good To Others' with a single-minded concentration.

The trouble was, that Wideshoes' idea of what was helpful did not always match with those who were on the receiving end.

Added to her endeavours were those of all the other Midi Cherubs, who were also taking every opportunity to do Good Deeds as the Community Challenge part of the Jacey Challenge. After a while, everyone was exhausted.

'Oh, Wideshoes,' sighed Roulus, as he used his great height to disentangle a kite and a distraught angel from a telinth. The angel had been flying by, thinking of other things, when a kite had zoomed into him. He had been so startled that it had knocked him right off course, and into the telinth.

'But little Katie couldn't get her kite up on her own. I was only trying to help. It was flying beautifully until A.Jo got in the way.'

'Yes, that was very kind of you. But, Wideshoes . . .' Roulus looked down, laughed his deep, rumbling laugh, and shook his head in mock despair. 'Oh, dear. What can I say? It *is* good to see you looking so much happier, little one.'

Wishbone found Wideshoes' new attitude very disconcerting. 'She keeps on bein' so nice 'n' polite to me,' he confided to Tictoc in a bewildered whisper, as Wideshoes apologised for accidentally interrupting him when he was speaking.

They were all in their secret hideout doing some more planning for the Jacey Challenge. Their marks were going really well, what with Wishbone's and Wideshoes' successful trip to Earth, and all the 'Good Deeds' they had all been doing. Even the marks they had taken off for the damage and inconvenience caused by Tictoc's experiment had been added back on, because of how pleased Roulus had been with the hard work Tictoc had put in to help put things right.

Roulus! Wideshoes remembered the Idea she had had a few days before. And it had not remained as just a plan. Now would be as good a time as any.

'Back soon. Things to do. People to see,' she said, and left.

Soon, she was back. 'O.K., you lot. Coming? I've got something really *reeelly* special sorted for you all. But we've got to go now.'

Tictoc did his usual 'I-don't-really-want-to-come-but-I'll-do-it-to-be-sociable' type sigh, and Wishbone his usual tease, but they came along nevertheless. Speck and Hattie were happy for a little diversion after all the serious discussion about the Challenge.

The four of them followed Wideshoes, their curiosity heightened as they approached the Cele-Park. It was here that the Archangels kept their huge Cele-Mobeels. Powerful enough to roar through space and beyond at fantastic speeds, and covering incredible distances in their patrolling of the heavens in order to keep them safe, the Cele-Mobeels were strictly out of bounds to unauthorised people – such as cherubs.

Even fun-loving Wishbone showed signs of

apprehension as they approached. 'I don' think we should be 'ere,' he said, nervously looking round.

'Trust me,' said Wideshoes, waving her hand airily.

The Mobeels towered over them like great metal sleeping giants as the cherubs followed Wideshoes, who was weaving her way purposefully amongst them.

Each Cele-Mobeel stood on its own launch-pad. Metal runners on the underside of the Mobeel fitted into metal channels to ensure a quick and smooth take-off.

Finally, she stopped by one of the biggest.

The cherubs stared up in awe at the mighty monster, the sweeping curved sides of which seemed to stretch up into the sky as far as they could see. It was a rich wine red in colour, with yellow ochre trimmings. The name of the owner was painted in large ochre letters on the side.

'Here we are,' said Wideshoes.

'R – O – U – L – U – S. Roulus,' spelled out Tictoc. '*Roulus?!?* What are you planning, Wideshoes? Oh, no. You're not going to play some stupid trick, are you? Actually, you can count me out, if you are.' Anxiety at what

Wideshoes had in mind had pulled him sharply out of his usual dreamy and detached state.

'And me,' said Speck and Wishbone and Hattie, all at the same time.

'Honest, you are pathetic,' said Wideshoes, in disgust. 'It's O.K.! I fixed it with Roulus. He's going to take us for a ride. I asked him.'

Wishbone looked at her with a new respect. ''ey! That were a bit clever of you. I've never b'n on a Celestial Space Ride. It'll be ace! So – where is 'e?'

'We're a bit early. Let's get in, then we'll be ready to go soon's he comes.'

Wideshoes was already climbing the vertical ladder that was permanently fixed to the side of the Cele-Mobeel. The others hesitated. Wideshoes looked down at them. 'Come on!' she called. 'It's O.K. *Reeelly* it is. Roulus won't mind.'

Once on board, they looked back over the side at where they had just been. The ground looked an impressive distance below. Then they turned their attention to the interior. They were near the rear and, in front of them, there were several rows of wine red padded seats for passengers. Large safety belts hung limp at the side of each seat, waiting to be clipped on.

They walked down the centre aisle to the front where two huge chairs were fixed to a dais. The chairs were confronted by a great instrument panel full of switches, dials, small computer panels, and other information sources.

Tictoc's eyes glistened with excitement as he looked at them. 'Oh, wow!' he breathed, scarcely able to believe what he was seeing. 'Oh, wow! Actually, this really is ace!'

Above the panel was an enormous window, which curved round at the sides for maximum vision. Hattie scrambled up onto one of the chairs, and looked out.

The great, curved, nose-cone of the Cele-Mobeel stretched out below like the beak of an eagle. Above, clouds moved lazily across a rather stormy-looking sky.

Several lights of the instrument panel were flashing. Roulus had obviously already been to prepare the Mobeel for take-off. The gentle throbbing of engines could be heard in the background during a pause in the cherubs' excited chatter. Wideshoes leaned dreamily against the instrument panel. She was feeling rather pleased with herself. This was going to be such fun.

Hattie's voice came from above her. 'That's strange. Those clouds have suddenly started moving ever so quickly past. Do you think there's going to be a storm?'

At that moment, the Cele-Mobeel began to vibrate gently.

'Must be,' said Tictoc. 'It's even making the Mobeel rock. I hope we can still go for the ride.'

Wishbone looked up at the sky, then down at Wideshoes. He pointed shakily at Wideshoes,

his eyes wide with horror. 'Git away from that panel!' he shouted. 'S'not the clouds – it's us! You must've knocked one of the starter switches on. You're jus' so *stoopid*!'

Wideshoes jumped away from the panel, as if she had been burned. 'Tictoc!' she screeched, '*Do* something!'

Tictoc looked wildly at the confusion of switches. More and more lights were starting to flash on the control panel. 'Me? – I don't know what to do!' he said helplessly, as the Cele-Mobeel accelerated through the darkening sky.

CHAPTER 12

Deep Space Danger!

Tictoc flicked randomly at one or two switches. There was a roar as the engines opened up to full throttle. The Cele-Mobeel gathered speed and began rocking violently.

'Oh, great! Brillian'!' shouted Wishbone, sarcastically.

Hattie, meanwhile, had grabbed the great steering wheel that was level with her, and was struggling to keep it from spinning first one way, then the other. The Cele-Mobeel steadied, but continued its now breakneck speed through the darkening sky. Soon, all the familiar areas were left far behind and the Mobeel, with its cargo of cherubs, was hurtling towards the distant stars that could be seen twinkling beyond the ominous, dark and heavy clouds.

Tictoc continued frantically to try to understand the instrument panel. But it was no use. The technology used had been very sophisticated indeed, and was far, far beyond the knowledge of a twelve-year-old, however interested in science. One random throwing of a switch did result in the Cele-Mobeel slowing down, but the strong winds that were buffeting the mighty machine made it roll and rock to such an alarming degree that Tictoc hastily returned the switch to its original position.

'What are we going to do?' sobbed Speck, now very frightened indeed, as the Cele-Mobeel gathered speed once more.

The others looked at him silently. Then Tictoc put his arm round his shoulders. 'Actually, it'll be O.K. We'll think of something.'

Speck looked up at him. 'What?' he asked.

Tictoc could not think of a reply. He felt very frightened, too.

Wideshoes' lower lip trembled. 'Sorry, everyone,' she said in a small voice. 'It's all my fault.'

At that moment, a great flash of lightning lit up the Mobeel, followed a moment later by an even greater crash of thunder. Speck whimpered quietly, and buried his face in Tictoc's shirt. It was not long before an immense storm was raging around them. Stabs of lightning were succeeded in quick succession by great rolls of thunder, followed by more lightning forking and crackling and snapping across the sky with terrifying force.

The Cele-Mobeel roared on.

As huge obstacles loomed up, and it seemed they would surely crash into them, the craft would swerve at the last minute and miraculously avoid them. 'Actually, there must be some sort of automatic, craft adjusting radar device, which activates when the engines start,' Tictoc said, glad to have some good news to share with the other terrified cherubs. 'I wonder if there's a homing device too?'

'Doesn't look like it,' said Wideshoes tremulously, as she gazed wide-eyed up at the overhead windows.

Time ceased to have any meaning. None of the cherubs had any idea how long they had been hurtling through the heavens – except that it felt like forever.

Far below on Earth, Helen and some of the other children involved in the disabled and able-bodied dance project, were sitting on one of the beds and gazing out at the stormy sky. The raging thunderstorm made it impossible to sleep, and it was comforting to be all together in the one room. Never before, they all agreed tremulously, had they ever seen such lightning or heard such thunder.

'Look!' said one. 'Shooting stars!' He pointed to two points of light rushing through the heavens, getting closer and closer to each other as each second passed.

They all watched, fascinated.

Some instinctive knowledge stirred deep down inside Helen. 'Wideshoes!' she murmured.

'Pardon?' said the girl next to her.

'Oh. Nothing.' But Helen just *knew*, as she continued to follow the progress of those points of light, that it all had something to do with her angel friends. She closed her eyes. 'Please, *please* take care of them,' she prayed silently.

Hattie, meanwhile, was still struggling to hold the wheel steady. 'Help me, someone!' she shrieked. 'I can't do this for too much longer!'

Wishbone scrambled up beside her, grabbed the wheel as well, and looked out at the pitch-black sky. Then he gasped. 'Look!' He pointed out of the window.

Hattie looked. There seemed to be a weird reflection of their own craft against the clouds. But no! It wasn't a reflection! Rocketing along and drawing closer by the minute, was a second Cele-Mobeel. In the front were two people.

She didn't recognise the woman pilot, with the long flowing hair. The other one was Roulus!

'Look! It's Roulus!' she screamed to the others. 'It's Roulus! It's all going to be O.K.!'

At that moment, his familiar voice boomed into the cabin. They all jumped and looked around, and then realised he was talking on the Intercom.

'Can you hear me? Are you all alright?'

'Yes!' they all shouted together.

'I repeat – can you hear me? Are you all alright?'

'Nod, Hattie! The Reply Intercom's not switched on in here,' shouted Wideshoes.

Hattie nodded frantically at the second Cele-Mobeel.

Again, Roulus's voice came over the Intercom. 'Tictoc – look at the Instrument Panel. On the right, is a red button, then a blue button, and then a switch. Do you see it?'

'Yes!' shouted Tictoc. Hattie nodded frantically again.

'Push the switch down.'

Tictoc pushed the switch down.

'I'm locking on to the remote-control system, and I will guide your Craft from here. We're going to head for ORES Daltus, one of our Outlying Refuelling and Emergency Stations. There both crafts will land. Rachella will bring this Cele-Mobeel back, and I will come aboard and pilot my Craft home. Hattie and Wishbone – there is no need for you to continue steering: that will happen automatically. Do you understand what is happening, all of you?'

Hattie and Wishbone looked enquiringly

down at the others, then nodded in unison.

It wasn't long before the two craft were landing at ORES Daltus. The immense skill of the two archangels – Rachella guiding her Cele-Mobeel, and Roulus operating the remote-control so accurately that the cherubs scarcely felt a bump as the craft touched the ground – brought them all down smoothly and safely.

A moment later, the great doors of the Cele-Mobeel swung open, and Roulus stood in their midst.

CHAPTER 13

Deep Space Rescue

'Oh, Roulus!' Wideshoes rushed over to give him a hug, but he brushed past her as he hurried over to the instrument panel. Scooping Hattie up in one arm, and Wishbone in the other, he set them down on the floor, then sat down in the chair on which they had been standing. Concentrating all his attention on the complex array of switches and lights and screens, he set to work. There was a roar as the engines once again opened up to full throttle.

Speck shuddered involuntarily. The noise was too closely linked with the terror that he and the others had been feeling, for what had seemed like forever. It would be some time before he could hear such a sound without shivering at the memories it stirred.

Soon, both craft were rushing through the heavens once more.

'We'll be home before long.' Roulus turned briefly, and smiled.

'Home! What a bootiful word!' thought Wishbone.

'Now, sit down, and put on those safety straps,' Roulus ordered.

The cherubs scurried to do as he said. Wideshoes giggled nervously, and Roulus turned his head once more in order to glare at her. 'This is no laughing matter, young lady,' he said sternly. 'You and I will be talking later.' Wideshoes hung her head, her lower lip wobbled and she brushed away a tear. She had never seen Roulus angry like this before, ever. Roulus was her special person. She adored him, and she couldn't bear to have so displeased him.

The children could feel the Cele-Mobeel begin to bank round steeply to the right.

Soon, the ice-cold temperature of the cabin gave way to a blissful warmth. Roulus had turned on the heating system. They had not realised how bitterly cold they were until then.

'One of you, come here please.'

'Can I help?' Wideshoes asked eagerly, desperate to make some positive contribution for a change.

'No. You stay right where you are. Hattie, come here please.'

Hattie went to Roulus's side. Keeping his eyes on the instruments, he bent over and lifted her up on to the chair beside him. 'See those lights there, and the buttons beside them?'

'Yes,' said Hattie, looking at the yellow, white and green colours that were flashing on and off, on and off.

'If they get duller, push in the right-hand button. If they get brighter, push in the left-hand button. If they are staying the same, don't do anything. Do you understand?'

'Yes,' said Hattie, feeling important.

'Tictoc, in that chest to your right are some blankets. In the one next to it, drinks and glucose sweets. Bring some here for Hattie, and then give the others some, will you please.'

Tictoc was a bit cross that he was having to give out the drinks, whilst Hattie was helping Roulus with the flying, but he did not dare say anything to that effect.

'Yes, Roulus,' he said meekly.

With drinks and sweets in their hands, and blankets over their knees, the cherubs began to enjoy themselves. Now Roulus was in control, they knew they were safe. The previous wild rocking and pitching of their outward journey was in total contrast to the smooth and steady ride with Roulus, who was renowned for his carefulness, safety and immense skill in operating these huge craft.

Wishbone looked out of the window beside him at the night sky rushing past. The stars were just blurs of light. 'We mus' be travellin' at a fantastic speed,' he thought sleepily.

Speck had curled up in his chair, pulled the blanket up to his chin, and was now fast asleep. His pack of juice had fallen to the floor, and was leaking slowly out.

Wideshoes undid her strap, and knelt down in order to clear it up. Unfortunately for her, Roulus glanced round at that moment. 'Wideshoes! I told you to sit still, with your strap on.'

'But I . . .'

'Just do as you are told, for once in your life, please.'

Wideshoes crept back to her chair, and strapped herself in. She pulled the blanket up to her chin. Some more tears trickled down her cheeks.

Wishbone smiled at her sympathetically. He had never seen Roulus this angry before, either. He would not like to be in Wideshoes' shoes – or boots – when they got back.

'Actually, it's a pity that the trip has gone so

terribly wrong,' thought Tictoc as he, too, stared out of the window. 'It's amazing to be flying through the night sky at this speed. If only we had waited for Roulus before climbing aboard. Now we'll probably never have another chance.' He could not somehow see Roulus wanting to take them anywhere, ever again.

Wishbone and Tictoc were also asleep by the time the Cele-Mobeel began to slow, then to come to rest on its landing stage.

Wideshoes, though, had felt too miserable to sleep. She was well aware that the terrible danger they had found themselves in was her fault. She would have liked this return journey to go on for ever; then she would not have to face the terrible wrath that she felt sure would soon be pouring over her head.

Roulus turned off the power, and stood up. 'Thank you, Hattie,' he smiled. 'Come on, let's get you and the others out of here. There will be a number of people very relieved indeed to see you all returned safely.' He slid back the door. Outside, a large group of people crowded round the base of the ladder. One by one the cherubs climbed down, then Roulus passed the still-sleeping Speck to willing hands. Finally, only Wideshoes was left.

'Well, Wideshoes?' he said, as he looked down at her.

CHAPTER 14

'That's It!'

Wideshoes hung her head. Roulus knelt down, cupped her face in his hands, and tilted her head back up. 'Look at me, Wideshoes,' he said firmly, as she continued to avoid his gaze.

Reluctantly, Wideshoes did as she was told. Roulus's dark piercing eyes looked deep into her sea-green ones. He loved all the cherubs in his charge with a fierce protective love, and would have done anything that was needed in order to protect them from any harm. But he had an extra-special soft spot in his heart for Wideshoes. Her harem-scarem ways, and trouble-prone activities despite all good intentions, reminded him of how he himself had been at her age. All he wanted to do now was to hug her and say how glad he was that she and the other cherubs were safe, but first he knew he had to make sure she understood just how much danger her actions had placed them all in.

'That was very, very irresponsible of you,' he said gravely. 'It might have been a very, very long time before we could have caught up with you. Fortunately, I arrived at the Launch Pad almost as soon as you had left. Fortunately, Rachella – one of our most skilled pilots and, believe you me, she had to be skilled in order to negotiate that craft at those speeds and in that weather – was nearby. My craft is one of the biggest and most powerful; Rachella's is the only other as powerful. If she had been out on patrol, or using it on some other task . . .'

Wideshoes listened to the list, her eyes filling once more with tears.

'I know,' she replied in a small voice. 'Thank you for rescuing us. And I'm so, so, so sorry . . . If anything had happened to you, Rachella or the others 'cause of me . . .' She slipped her arms round his neck and clung to him, her tears soaking his shoulder.

Roulus comfortingly patted her back and stroked her curls alternately, then scooped her up and carried her out of the cabin and down the stairs. Wideshoes kept her face buried in his shoulder. She was too ashamed and embarrassed to look at all the people she knew would be there.

Then she heard her name being softly called, by a voice she knew very well indeed.

'Jacey!' She looked up. He was standing at the bottom of the steps, the still-soundly sleeping Speck in one arm, with the other placed around Wishbone, Hattie and Tictoc. In his smile of delight there was no anger, only relief and love.

Wideshoes could hardly bear it. It would almost have been easier to have some awful, terrible punishment. She gulped. 'I'm truly, terribly, most awfully sorry,' she said in a tear-laden small voice.

Roulus set her down in front of Jacey, who managed somehow to extend his embrace of the others to include her as well. 'I know,' he said simply.

He turned to Roulus, and smiled. 'Thank you Roulus, my dear friend, for bringing them safely back.'

He looked at the children. 'All is well. We must give you something to eat; you must be so hungry. Come along, everyone – we must have a party to celebrate the return of our little ones.'

Tictoc stiffened at being called little – but then decided that perhaps he didn't mind too much after all as it was Jacey who had said it.

The celebrations went on well into the night as all of heaven rejoiced at the safe return of the cherubs. The account of Roulus's and Rachella's daring rescue bid was told over and over, and it was generally agreed that this latest example of their bravery would be a fitting one to add to all the other courageous deeds that had made their names so renowned and revered everywhere. Hattie was heroine of the hour, as the story of her wrestling with the wheel was also told and retold.

And Wideshoes was not left out. 'Everyone's

bein' so nice to me,' she thought miserably. 'I don't deserve it.' But, gradually, their warmth melted the sadness in her heart and she began to enjoy the party with more and more of her usual zest.

Goodie watched Wideshoes and Gang at the centre of all the attention, and felt envious. 'I don't know what all the fuss is about,' she sniffed to her friend. 'Whatever she does, she gets forgiven in the end. It's not fair.'

Wideshoes turned at that moment, and caught Goodie's gaze. 'Everyone's being so nice to me, I must be nice back to everyone as a kind of thank you – even Goodie,' she thought. 'Hiya!' she called, smiling brightly.

Goodie sniffed again, and turned away. 'Why is it that Wideshoes is so popular with everyone? Even when she's done yet another stupid thing,' Goodie thought in her turn. Though Goodie would never have admitted it, even to her best friend, she secretly wished she had Wideshoes' gift for getting on with all sorts of people.

Tictoc and Wishbone, meanwhile, were in great demand to give first-hand accounts of all that had happened.

Speck slept through it all curled up in Jacey's arm who, mysteriously, did not seem to tire of his burden, even though the party continued for many hours.

A few days later, the Gang were in their secret hideout. They were despondently trying to calculate how many marks they should deduct, because of the Cele-Mobeel incident, from those previously gained for the Jacey Challenge.

'Soz, everyone,' said Wideshoes meekly, as they finally fixed on a rather large number.

Tictoc chewed the pencil he was using to write with, clicked his tongue thoughtfully, and frowned. 'Actually, *actually* I think we should take some marks off for me, too,' he said eventually. 'I'm the eldest after all, and I should've acted more responsibly instead of just going along with it, even though I didn't agree.'

The others argued against him, but he was insistent. They took off some more marks eventually, then looked gloomily at the result.

Wishbone spoke, sounding unusually depressed. 'None 'f us – 'part from Wideshoes who's done 'ers – has even fixed on what Pers'nal Challenge we're goin' to do yet, either. We're makin' a real mess 'f all of this. Bet we come last. The points we got for 'attie bein' an 'eroine, we've lost by Tictoc wantin' to be a martyr.' He pulled out his flute, played a few mournful notes, then stopped.

'When's 'n angel not 'n angel?' he asked, then answered himself. 'When it's Wideshoes – yeah!'

Wideshoes looked at him speechless and wide-eyed.

'Sorry,' he said penitently. 'Only teasin'.'

'But that's it!' said Wideshoes excitedly. 'For our Group Challenge we could put on a Show. We'll get heaps of marks for that. It'll be ace!'

'Oh, yes!' said Hattie, catching her friend's enthusiasm. 'That'd fit in fine with the rules, wouldn't it?' She went over to where they had pinned up Tictoc's scrap of paper about the Challenge, and read out, '"The Group Challenge: – Join together with several other cherubs, and work together on a project of some kind: it is your choice as to what sort of project." You could play the flute, Wishbone.'

'*An*' tell some awful jokes, I 'spect,' added Speck.

Even Tictoc agreed, and they began enthusiastically and excitedly planning the contents of their Show, when and where it should be held, who to invite, and so on.

Little did they know that, precisely at the same time and by a dreadful coincidence, Goodie and Co were also engaged in planning a Show. And that the date, venue and time were exactly the same as those finally decided upon by Wideshoes and the Gang.

CHAPTER 15

Midnight Boat Ride

It was early evening by the time the Gang crawled, bleary-eyed, out of the hideout.

'Let's go to the Lake 'n' see if Peter's there,' suggested Wishbone.

He was, and was just about to cook something to eat over a fire he had built at the water's edge. 'Care to join me?' he asked. 'I've got plenty.' He loaded more food onto the grid over the fire without bothering to wait for an answer. After a few minutes, during which the Gang sat without speaking, watching Peter cooking and gazing into the flames, Peter looked sideways at Wishbone. 'You're unusually quiet,' he observed. 'In fact, you all are.'

He and Wishbone were the best of friends, and Peter often took the young cherub on sailing trips, sharing his favourite pastime, over a day or two, or three. He knew the lad very well, and could read his moods with pinpoint accuracy. Just as Roulus was to Wideshoes, and Francis to Speck, so St. Peter was to Wishbone.

As they sat round the fire, eating the food

with their fingers in the gathering twilight, the flickering flames cast lights and shadows on them, and they shared their problems. Peter listened without interrupting. He knew all about the Cele-Mobeel incident – who didn't? – but he still let them tell it all in their own words, well knowing how just the sharing of something often brings its own solution.

As they talked he saw how much their bubbling confidence and belief in themselves had been shaken, and he began to tell them about how once, long ago and when he was still on Earth, his belief in himself had been shattered.

'I was a broken, frightened man,' he said. 'A trembling wreck of a person. You may not believe it, but I was. Indeed I was.'

The cherubs looked incredulously at the big, muscular, bearded man.

'I'd been so cocky and sure of myself that, whatever I chose to do I could do but then, just at the most important moment when I could have proved it, I let him down. I betrayed him by saying I had never known him.' Peter's voice shook even now at the memory.

'Who's "him?"' whispered Speck to Tictoc.

'Jacey,' came the whispered reply.

Peter looked into the flickering flames, then blinked fiercely a few times before continuing. 'But he forgave me. And from that moment on, I really started to become the person I had always imagined I was – but, in fact, hadn't been.

'So, you see, if you are sorry for your mistakes, and are prepared to learn from them, you will quite probably end up doing much better than you ever could have before. Mistakes and disasters can sometimes actually be good for you. It all depends upon what you do with them, and how you use them.'

He paused for a while to let his words sink in, then smiled around at the thoughtful cherubs. 'How's about a bit of a starlight boat ride then before you go to bed? And then we can talk some more about the Jacey Challenge, and what you might each do.

'First, though, we'd better let someone know what we're going to do, else Roulus might stage another rescue bid.' Peter concentrated deeply for a moment, in order to send a message by mental telepathy, then the Gang helped him to push the boat off the shore and they all climbed in.

Peter had an amazing way with him. By the time they had landed back on shore in the early morning light he had drawn out of each of them what they felt they wanted, and what they felt they ought, to do for their Personal Challenge – helping them to put together dreams and reality into something possible, challenging and creative.

'The ideas and the solutions are all there, locked up inside each one of you,' he said. 'I'm just helping you find the key to open them up.'

Wishbone lay sprawled in the bow of the boat, trailing his hand through the water. He loved being with Peter, in his craft or on the lakeside, learning about boats and how to sail and navigate; how to skim stones across the water so that they bounced many times before finally disappearing (so far, Wishbone's best score had been ten, but Peter could manage an amazing twenty-one); and talking with Peter, and hearing his tales.

Now Peter prodded him with his toe. 'Come on, young fellow-me-lad,' he said gruffly, 'I need your help to sail this thing, with all these landlubbers on board.'

The moon and the stars looked at themselves reflected in the inky-black water, making dancing slivers of light as they did so. The water slapped and slurped against the sides of the boat.

Speck crept a bit closer to Peter, taking comfort from his big solid presence. 'Scared of the dark, young Speck?' Peter enquired softly. 'So brave and courageous with animals, even the great Zanton, yet frightened of the dark? Hmm. Do you think Zanton's afraid of the dark?'

'Oh, no,' said Speck. 'Zanton's not scared of nothing. If I was like Zanton, I 'spect I wouldn't be frightened of nothing neither.'

'There you are,' said Peter. 'I think you might just have found your Personal Challenge. Speak to Francis. He'll know how to help you.'

Some time later, they reefed in the sails and tied the tiller, then lay on their backs looking dreamily up at the stars, letting the boat drift at its will as they talked and laughed. It was a magical feeling, surrounded by the still, dark beauty of the night.

Then Peter told them stories of the time he and Jacey and others had walked throughout the Holy Land, preaching and teaching, healing and raising.

The cherubs alternately listened, and dozed, as sleep insisted on closing their eyelids.

In between his storytelling, Peter talked in soft tones to each one in turn about what they might hope to do for their own Personal Challenges.

'Well,' said Tictoc frowning and thinking deeply, 'as it's supposed to be a challenge I suppose, actually, that I should do something really different from science. Like something to do with Nature for instance. But I don't know, I can't seem somehow to get all interested in Nature like Wishbone is. Oh, I don't know . . . I suppose I ought . . . Yes. Nature I think, actually. I don't know what, though.'

Peter thought for a while, then suggested Tictoc joined him on an expedition he was soon to lead. 'You'll learn all about Nature on *that*, my lad!' he chuckled.

Hattie confided in a whisper: 'Although Roulus said that what I did on the Cele-Mobeel could count as my personal challenge, I thought that I'd like to do something else – so's I can earn some more marks for the Gang. We've lost rather a lot, you see,' she added ruefully. 'But I can't think what to do.'

'Is there something about yourself that you wish was different?' probed Peter gently.

Hattie thought for a moment. 'Oh, yes,' she said. 'I get really shy about all sorts of things. I wish I was like Wideshoes. She never lets being shy get in the way of anything she wants to say or do. But me – I get all worried I'll look silly, and that stops me. I wish I was more like her.'

'Don't be,' replied Peter. 'Be yourself. You are you, not Wideshoes. What's right for her may not be right for you. Concentrate on being yourself, then you'll be the best you can be.'

'But how . . . ?'

'Something'll turn up, you mark my words, young lady,' promised Peter mysteriously, 'now that you've decided.'

Wishbone, meanwhile, was feeling jealous of Tictoc. He had been coiling up some ropes nearby, and had overheard Peter inviting Tictoc on the expedition. He already knew all about the trip, and he had been cherishing a secret hope until now that Peter would take *him*. In fact, he had assumed Peter would, and he had been really looking forward to it. Now, he stared moodily out over the water and absentmindedly juggled with some pebbles he had found in his pocket.

Peter watched Wishbone through half-closed eyes, and understood. 'And you, First Mate, what are you going to do?' It was Peter's special name for him when they were out in the boat on one of the Lakes or Waterways.

Wishbone shrugged. 'Dunno,' he answered. 'Clown aroun', I s'pose. That's all ev'ryone seems to think I'm good for.' He continued to look moodily out into the darkness, and Peter let him be for the moment. He turned to Wideshoes. 'I suppose you did your Personal Challenge by going to help Helen?'

Wideshoes nodded. 'Mmmm,' she said. Like Hattie, though, Wideshoes had been wanting to do something else as well. 'It's a lot of my fault that the Gang's lost so many marks, and I do so want to make it up to them,' she thought. 'I'll see Roulus first of anyone, and ask what he thinks of my plan.' However, she did not share any of this with Peter.

Peter waited for a moment in case Wideshoes wanted to expand on her reply of 'Mmm', then turned his attention back to Wishbone. 'Three days from now, I'm trying out a very special boat on Storm Lake, testing it for its strength and reliability. I need you to come as First Mate. Be ready at sunrise. I'll pick you up then. O.K.?'

Wishbone nodded, but didn't say anything. A while later though, the sound of his flute drifted across the water, and Peter smiled to himself in the depths of his great, shaggy beard.

CHAPTER 16

The Gang Meets the Challenge

Wideshoes lay on her stomach, chin cupped in her hands, watching Roulus as he worked.

'Stop sniffing. Young ladies don't sniff,' he said, looking up and smiling. Wideshoes grinned back, so happy that Roulus and she were best friends again.

'I'm glad you are here,' he continued. 'I wanted to speak to you about that Cele-Mobeel trip.'

Wideshoes' sunny smile faded, and a look of deep dismay replaced it. Roulus laughed. 'No, I'm not going to tell you off again. I mean a trip that *I* take you on. I promised, and I can't break a promise now, can I. Tomorrow, I have to do a patrol of the Mellem Way. I'll pick you all up after school, and you can come along with me, if you'd like to.'

'Oh, Roulus! That'll be ace! Thank you. Thank you! Just wait until I tell the others!'

'Now. What was it you really came to see me about?'

Wideshoes told him what she had been

thinking; about the marks lost for the Cele-Mobeel incident; how she'd wanted to do an extra Personal Challenge to get extra marks, and so make it up to the others; how she felt she ought to do something she really disliked as that would be good for her – and get more marks. But what should she do, and could he help her choose the exact thing please?

Roulus listened as the words tumbled out. The rules were that the idea had to come from the cherub herself, or himself – and it had. Wideshoes just needed his help to find exactly the right thing. He smiled. 'Leave it to me. I think I can promise to find you something you will really dislike very much indeed.'

Wideshoes looked at him suspiciously. 'Not too, *too* nasty,' she said cautiously. 'Just kind of middling . . .'

The Cele-Mobeel Trip was a great success. The Mellem Way was one of the most beautiful, and they did not know which way to look first as there was so much to see and to wonder at. Roulus explained some of the mysteries behind what they saw. He told them a little about how to navigate your way around the heavens in the daytime, using the colours of the sky, the cloud shapes, and other guides. He was immensely skilled at handling the huge craft, which glided smoothly through the heavens under his expert hand, and each of the cherubs in turn was allowed to assist him in piloting.

The sun was setting as they returned, its light forming a golden road along which they rode back to the landing stage.

The next day, Peter and Wishbone went to Storm Lake to try out the new boat and to put it through its paces. Whilst there, an unexpected thing happened.

Storm Lake lived up to its name, and a sudden storm began to brew whilst they were far out from shore. Hurrying to reef in a sail, Peter seemed to stumble. He collapsed in a heap at the back of the boat. 'Sorry, First Mate. You'll have to take the boat in,' he shouted over the rising wind. 'I've done something to my leg.'

Wishbone rushed over to his friend. 'Where's it 'urt?' he asked anxiously, tentatively feeling Peter's leg.

Peter obliged with a loud 'Ouch!' followed by 'Don't bother with me, lad, bother with the boat. It's up to you now to get us home safely.'

Wishbone felt a rush of panic as he looked at the fast-gathering storm clouds. Then he looked at Peter, who was sitting there grimacing, and obviously in a lot of pain.

He had to get his beloved friend back as soon as possible, so that he could have his leg seen to. It was up to him.

Wishbone firmly set his panic on one side, and concentrated on remembering all that Peter had taught him about sailing on rough waters. Peter shouted a few instructions where necessary, but he seemed too preoccupied with his pain most of the time to be able to do more than that.

Soon the boat was pitching and tossing, and Wishbone rushed hither and thither, reefing in a sail here, letting one out there, lashing the tiller so that they did not spin round in circles. Meanwhile, the storm crashed and raged around them, as they slowly crept nearer and nearer to shore. The rain was pouring down now, penetrating their waterproofs, and they were soaked through and shivering. Visibility was down to just a few metres, and Wishbone had finally to rely on compass bearings to navigate a route to the shore.

It seemed forever before Wishbone finally was able to jump overboard and push the boat to the water's edge.

People soon appeared, helped pull the boat up, and assisted Peter out. Peter seemed much more intent upon telling everyone about the heroic efforts of 'my First Mate' than in going to get his leg seen to. Considering the amount of pain he had said he was in, he seemed remarkably agile.

'P'r'aps e's relieved to be back,' thought Wishbone, as he watched him. 'Funny, thought it were 'is other leg that got injured.'

'Well done, lad! Knew you could do it!' Peter slapped him on the back, before beginning to hobble up the beach dragging his left leg. Then he turned. 'Oh, yes. By the way. I think you can count that as a Personal Challenge confronted, and excellently fulfilled. Top marks. Definitely top marks. I'll make sure Roulus knows.' He winked, then continued on up the beach, this time dragging his right leg.

At that precise moment, Hattie was in Sacc's office. The Senior Angel was telling her about the large and Very Important Conference that was to be held in order to look at the arrangements for the reception, care and nurture of all the young arrivals in heaven.

Very many people would be there, and Sacc wanted Hattie to accompany her, to talk to the entire gathering about being a new arrival: about the care she had received, and any suggestions she might have to make it even better.

Hattie thought of her conversation with Peter in the boat. She knew she had to say yes. Not for Sacc's sake – although she did want to be of any help she could – but for her own sake. 'You can't go round it, you gotta go through it,' she murmured to herself, remembering one of the campfire songs she used to sing, about facing problems and difficult situations, when at summer camps on Earth.

Wideshoes stood in the middle of the clamouring infants, looked around her in the deepest dismay and then glared at Roulus, who chuckled merrily. 'But I don't even *like* children of this age,' she protested. 'Well, that is – I kind 'f, sort 'f, like them – but I'm *no good* with them. Not like Hattie is. She should be doing this. She's kind and good and patient and gentle . . .'

A tiny child tugged at Wideshoes' sleeve, and pointed to her shorts which, from the smell, obviously were in serious need of attention. 'Oh, Roulus!' wailed Wideshoes.

'I did what you asked,' he said heartlessly.

'Yes, but . . .'

'They really need your help. They're very short-staffed in this area at the moment for various reasons.'

'How *long*?'

'Till Christmas.'

'Christmas?!' she shrieked. 'Oh, Roulus! I hate you!'

'No you don't. You're just cross with me because I have given you a real challenge. See what you can make of it. Anyway, I was only teasing. You can finish on Sunday.'

'Oh, Roulus. Do I have to stay?'

'Well, if you don't want those extra marks, that's up to you. No one is forcing you.'

'Roulus –'

'Yes?'

'I love you really.'

Roulus smiled down at her, and then disappeared.

Another infant tugged at Wideshoes' other sleeve. He also appeared to have similar problems to the first infant. Wideshoes sighed. 'I'd better get heaps 'n' heaps 'n' *heaps* of marks for this,' she muttered to herself, as she gingerly investigated the problem.

Chapter 17

'We Dun It!'

'If you want the secret of Zanton's heart, you must hear it from him,' said Francis.

Speck frowned. 'I 'spect I don't understand lion talk,' he said, puzzled.

'Yes, you do. You and I and lamb are Zanton's best friends. Best friends understand each other. But they don't need words, do they? Just being together is enough.'

Speck *thought* he understood.

'If you agree,' continued Francis, 'I'll arrange for you to come and stay for a few days with Zanton. It'd mean you missing a day or two of school, but I daresay Sacc won't mind too much as it is for a good reason. What do you think?'

'Ooh, yes! Yes, please!' Speck's eyes were round with excitement.

And so it was that Speck did just that. For several days he walked with Zanton; rode on his back; lay resting his head, with lamb, against his great mane; whispered long conversations into his ear, and listened to Zanton's replies. He even slept with him, curled up close and snuggled down between his great front paws, with lamb and Francis nearby.

'And did you learn the secret of Zanton's great and fearless heart?' asked Francis as they ate their last breakfast together.

'Yes. I 'spect I did,' said Speck. 'He does get scared. But he thinks of his father, who was the greatest lion ever. Then he's not so scared no more. When I get scared, I shall think of Zanton, and then I 'spect I won't be so scared no more, neither.'

'What else did you learn?' asked Francis.

'Secrets,' said Speck mysteriously. 'Lots of secrets. But Zanton says I mustn't tell.' And he shut his lips firmly together.

And Tictoc? Well, it would take a whole book on its own to recount all his adventures with Peter on that Expedition, and so the details of what happened must be told another time. Suffice it to say that he was away considerably longer than intended.

As Peter had promised, he did learn a great deal about Nature – and about a number of other things as well.

Hattie went to the Conference, was nearly sick with shyness and nerves but, when she got up to

144

talk, found her nerves just melted away. Everyone listened intently, and there was much scribbling of notes. When Hattie sat down they all clapped enthusiastically and for a very long time.

Afterwards, someone who had been a Very Famous Actress Indeed on Earth, swept up to Hattie. 'Darling!' she declared dramatically, 'You have *the* most divine speaking voice – and, of course, you look *absolutely* heavenly, as I'm sure you have been told on many occasions. I should so like to take you under my wing, and train you in the Art of Dramatic Speaking and Acting. You have *such* potential! What do you say? May I speak to Sacc?'

Hattie was wide-eyed with surprise, both at what was being said, and at the buzz of excitement the actress's words gave her. It was like a moment of truth: as if she'd always wanted this, but had never known it until now. 'Yes. Oh, yes! I-I'd really like that. Th-thank you,' she stammered.

'Oh! Those eyes! Just too divine,' cooed the older angel. And then she swept away. A few moments later she was deep in animated conversation with Sacc.

Christmas was fast approaching, and the

others waited impatiently for Tictoc's return. They couldn't continue planning the Show until he was back.

Meanwhile, still unknown to the Gang, Goodie and Co's Show was coming along very well indeed. They had sent out invitations, and were now busily making costumes and stage backdrops.

Wishbone struggled with his recurring feelings of jealousy when they heard that the Expedition's return had, yet again, been delayed. 'I bet 'e's 'avin 'n ace time. I wish, I wish it was me,' he confided to Hattie.

At last Tictoc was home again, but was strangely reluctant to talk about the trip other than to say, 'Actually, it was absolutely totally amazing. Brill, in fact.'

The day after his return, the Gang were sitting in their hideout. They had all done well with their Personal Challenges and their total marks, agreed with Roulus, were looking very satisfactory.

'Please, Wideshoes, no more disasters,' they begged her.

At this she had looked very offended, but just said 'Huh!' which, for her, was *very* restrained.

'We've got some planning t' do,' she now declared. 'Really mega-serious planning. We're in with a chance now, and we just gotta beat Goodie and Co. Wonder what they're doing for their Group Challenge. Does anyone know?'

No one did.

'I wonder how we can find out,' Wideshoes frowned, chewing her lip.

'It's not meant to be a competition,' Tictoc reminded her, yet again. 'Just a challenge to ourselves.'

'Yes. Well. I know. Even so . . .' muttered Wideshoes.

Truth to tell, they were all very much wanting to be the best of all the cherubs – and especially to beat Goodie and Co. However, as the marks were not going to be published so Roulus had assured them all, how would they know? But as Wideshoes had said, 'Even so . . .'

They were soon absorbed in their planning. All of a sudden, it seemed, as is the way with things if you struggle and persevere long enough, their pencil chewing and writing, discussions and arguments, had paid off. Everything was fitting together nicely.

'We dun' it!' cheered Wishbone, turning a

celebratory cartwheel, but also succeeding in kicking one of the wonky shelves with the drinks and crisps off the wall as he did so. 'Oops!'

Over the following days, they decided where they were going to hold the Show, and began making preparations.

Tictoc checked out the lighting, and planned to add his own home-made rainbow ones. 'Is that wise?' Hattie asked anxiously, remembering the Walkway Incident.

Wishbone, Hattie and Speck painted some cloths to hang as backdrops. Hattie wrote out the programme with copies for their main guests: Sacc, Roulus, Francis, Peter and their Most Special Guest, Jacey. They had all been sent invitations, and each had replied that they were looking forward to coming very much indeed.

By now, the Gang were getting really excited. And they weren't the only ones. Dotted around wherever you went there seemed to be small knots of cherubs whispering conspiratorially, rushing around purposefully, or looking a bit desperate, as plans went awry last minute and as the Christmas deadline crept ever closer.

CHAPTER 18

Problems and Solutions

Ten days before the Show, Wideshoes and Gang went to have a run-through at the venue they had chosen.

Goodie and Co were there.

'What are *you* doing here?' asked Tictoc, surprised. Actually, this is *our* place.'

'No, it's not,' said Goodie, in her usual superior voice. '*We're* doing a Show here next week.'

'When?'

'On the Sunday evening.'

'But you can't, 'cos we are!' exclaimed Wideshoes.

'No, you're not. We are!'

'No, you aren't!'

'Yes, we are!'

The argument looked set to go on all night.

'We were here first.'

'No, you weren't. We were.'

'We've sent out invitations!'

'So have we!'

Deadlock. A temporary halt was called as it

was time for supper. 'What *are* we going to do?' sighed Hattie, whilst they were eating.

'I know. Let's go and see Roulus. He'll sort them out,' suggested Wideshoes.

'Actually, I don't think he will,' said Tictoc.

He was right. 'You will have to sort this out between you,' said Roulus, 'and come to some agreement.' Wideshoes tried wheedling, but he was adamant.

'Told you,' said Tictoc after they had left.

Suddenly, Hattie began to jump up and down. 'I've got it! I've got it!' she said excitedly. 'Let's stick the two shows together!'

'Never!' said Wideshoes.

'I 'spect Hattie's right,' volunteered Speck. As quite often happened, it was because Speck thought it was a good suggestion that the others were finally persuaded. As the youngest, his opinions were respected.

A meeting with Goodie and Co was arranged, who agreed with the proposal.

Goodie and her friends had been having equally agitated discussions about what to do, and had been about to make a similar suggestion – though Goodie could not quite bring herself to tell Wideshoes this.

The next thing was to try to put together the two very different programmes.

Goodie and Co's programme looked like this:

And Wideshoes and Gang's programme looked like this:

After a great deal of discussion and argument, an agreement was reached, and the final programme looked like this:

THE CHERUB THEATRE COMPANY
PROUDLY PRESENTS:

DANCE: GOODIE & CO. (MUSIC BY WISHBONE)
POETRY: HATTIE
DANCE MIME & MUSIC: THE C.T.C
ACROBATICS & JOKES: WISHBONE
FASHION SHOW: GOODIE & CO

INTERVAL!
(C.T.C FIZZ & ANGEL CAKES WILL BE SERVED)

A HEAVENLY SKETCH: TICTOL & SPECK
THE CHRISTMAS STORY: THE C.T.C
JACEY'S SONG: WIDESHOES & BAND
WITH THE C.T.C DANCERS.

News that Wideshoes and Gang and Goodie and Co were working together on a show spread like wildfire, and tickets were selling very fast. Everyone wanted to be there. Though whether it was to see the show itself, or Goodie and Wideshoes on the same stage at the same time, was not clear.

It was Friday, two days before the Show, and

Wideshoes and Gang were rehearsing the Christmas Story.

'Oh!' wailed Wideshoes, clasping her hand to her brow dramatically. 'It's just not right somehow.'

''s borin',' said Wishbone. 'Not the story, but the way we're doin' it.'

'We used to do a Nativity Play like this every year in church,' murmured Hattie dreamily. 'It was really, really nice.' She paused, and looked at the others. 'I've just thought – they'll be doing it tomorrow. Same weekend as us.'

'Let's stop now,' suggested Tictoc, 'and come back to it tomorrow. Maybe we're just tired.'

Later that evening, Wideshoes asked Hattie all about the play her church used to do.

'I wish, I wish I could see it,' sighed Wideshoes. Then she looked thoughtful. 'I wonder . . .'

Hattie looked at her horrified. 'Wideshoes! You wouldn't!'

'Nobody need know,' said Wideshoes. 'I'd only be gone a few hours. I'll be back 'fore I'm missed. And it'd be ever so helpful to get some ideas to make our play a bit better. It's my 'sponsibility as Pr'ducer. Don't you dare tell. Promise?'

CHAPTER 19

'I'll Be Back Before I'm Missed'

It was a cold, crisp day. Wideshoes stood outside the church door, and watched everyone going in before entering herself. Invisible, she stood by the staging that had been erected at the front, and watched the last-minute preparations in fascination.

Young girls and boys in what looked like sheets, with tinselly stuff round their heads, more children in dressing gowns and tea-towels, and yet more in colourful garments and crowns and carrying various shaped boxes wrapped in glittering paper, were being chivvied hither and thither by a young woman dressed in a green shirt with a white collar, black jeans and a matching denim jacket. Elegant black leather boots completed the outfit.

Wideshoes approved the style.

A harassed-looking man rushed up to the woman. 'I'm so sorry, Vicar,' he gasped, out of breath, 'but Tommy's got Chicken Pox. He's absolutely covered from head to toe in spots. There's no way he will be able to play Angel

Gabriel today!'

'Oh, no!' The Vicar cast her eyes heavenwards in utter dismay. 'Oh, Lord! Give me inspiration!' She turned, and her jaw dropped.

'Good heavens! I don't believe it! The answer to my prayer! Where *on earth* did you spring from? My dear, what *wonderful* wings! They're just *so* authentic. You just must take Tommy's place. Would you? Do please say you will.'

Wideshoes looked behind her, then realised in horror that the young woman was talking to her. She must have become visible! 'Yes. No. Well. That is – I – ,' she stammered.

' . . . don't know the part,' supplied the young woman. 'Don't worry. You just stand there looking angelic. I'll whisper the words from the side, and you can repeat them. Please do say yes, and save the day for us.'

A dazed Wideshoes was led to the staging.

By now, all the audience was seated and waiting expectantly for the play to begin. Someone slipped a long sheet thing over Wideshoes' head, then she was pushed on to the stage.

'Raise your hands!' hissed a voice, 'and say: "Greetings! I bring you tidings of great joy."'

Wideshoes raised her hands, and composed

her face in what she hoped looked like an angelic expression. What *were* the words? 'Um – Greetings!' she said. 'I bring you tidelings that – er – will annoy . . .'

A muted ripple of laughter ran round the audience.

Meanwhile, in heaven, Wideshoes' absence had been discovered. An agitated Hattie was saying to Sacc and Roulus, 'But I promised!'

'Hattie,' said Sacc gently. 'I release you from that promise. Wideshoes may be in danger. We *have* to know where she has gone, and quickly. Roulus could use his psychic powers to locate her, but that would take time. Please *do* tell us.'

'Oh, dear!' Hattie looked at them both, and struggled between breaking a promise, and the possibility that Wideshoes might be in danger and so would need help. She decided she had to say.

Buildings on Earth were no problem to Roulus, and he entered the church through the three-feet-thick walls with ease.

Wideshoes was well into her part by now. ' . . . a Saviour who is Christ the Lord,' she declared, raising her arms high.

Invisible to everyone else, Roulus swooped

down, grasped Wideshoes' hands in his and, together, they ascended towards the church rafters. The last the astounded Vicar and audience saw of Wideshoes were her kicking boots, as she disappeared from view.

Roulus let go of one hand and transferred his grip to around Wideshoes' waist, and she completed the journey in an undignified manner tucked under his arm. He set her down.

'Wideshoes!' he thundered. 'What *did* you think you were doing?'

Wideshoes gulped. 'I was being Angel Gabriel. I was doing research for our Show.'

'An angel was about the last thing you were being,' said Roulus, his anger beginning to melt at the comical sight of Wideshoes dressed in a sheet.

At that moment Hattie, Tictoc, Wishbone, Speck and Goodie and Co all ran up. They stood staring at Wideshoes, and Goodie giggled. 'Why are you dressed in a sheet?' she asked.

Wideshoes glared at her, looked down at herself and giggled too. 'This is what people on Earth think angels wear,' she gurgled.

They all laughed until the tears ran down their faces.

CHAPTER 20

The Cherub Theatre Company Proudly Presents . . .

The Show was going better than they dared dream it would.

If they had been able to influence it, the moon could not have been more perfectly positioned: a full round creamy-orange orb, shining from behind the stage and in full view of the audience. Many stars added their own sparkling light to the artificial ones on stage, which was a raised grassy area at one end of a large clearing. Tictoc's lights were a great success and had worked perfectly.

Another source of radiant and dazzling light came from where one particular person, the special guest of honour, sat.

The clearing was packed, and they had been an appreciative audience – laughing at Wishbone's jokes, and applauding his acrobatics – hushed, and listening intently, when Hattie recited her poetry – individuals ruefully recognised themselves, but were the loudest to clap at the accuracy of the imitations, when Tictoc and Speck did a sketch taking off various inhabitants of heaven – loved the dancing, music and mime – and oohed and aahed at Goodie and Co's fashion show.

The C.T.C. (Cherubs Theatre Company) Fizz, and the angel cakes, had been much enjoyed by everyone during the Interval.

Now it was time for the Nativity Play.

Jacey sat forward in his chair, and listened and watched intently. There was a faraway, dreamy look in his eyes . . .

The whole Theatre Company was taking part. Hattie and Tictoc played Mary and Joseph. The others played the shepherds and kings, admiring and worshipping the baby (borrowed for the occasion from the Nursery where Wideshoes had done her Personal Challenge), and placing gifts before him.

The Tableau froze.

Wishbone walked in playing his flute. His gift to the Babe was the haunting soft melody he had composed specially, and now played. The tune ended and there was a moment of breath-held stillness.

Then, dignified and majestic, in padded Zanton with Speck on his back, and his lamb friend trotting by his side. They, too, joined the Tableau gathered around and worshipping the Infant Jesus.

You could have heard a pin drop, so hushed was the audience. That eternal moment in history had been captured perfectly by the cherubs, and there was such a great sense of awe throughout the open-air theatre you could almost reach out and touch it.

There was a silence rather than a clapping of the audience's appreciation, which seemed right, as the lights dimmed and the Tableau quietly left the stage.

A few moments later, the strobes began sending their multi-coloured beams skimming round and round the open-air theatre, and the stage lights came full on.

Wideshoes was centre stage, feet planted squarely. She was holding the stand microphone at an angle across her gyrating body, and was shaking her head round and round and round. In a curve behind her stood Wishbone playing his flute; Tictoc plucking a double bass made from an orange box, a pole and taut wire; Speck and one of Goodie's group – a girl of about his age – were rhythmically tapping a home-made xylophone composed of various jars filled to different levels with water.

Hattie and Goodie stood at a second microphone, shaking maracas made out of dried beans in tins. They were also acting as the backing singers. The rest of the Theatre Company were fanned out across the stage, dressed in colourful outfits, dancing in time to the music.

'O – O – O – Oh, Jay – Cee!
You are
so a-cee,' Wideshoes shrilled.
'Yeah! Yeah! Yeah!' sang Goodie and Hattie.
'There is
no pla-cee
where you
are not!' Wideshoes continued, giving it all she'd got.
'Yeah! Yeah! Yeah!' sang Hattie and Goodie.
'Jay-Cee
we adore you!
There is no more yo-ou
could do-oo
for us
than
you
do-ooo-ooo!'

Wideshoes gyrated and pirouetted and shook her head around until every curl seemed to be bouncing in a variety of directions. Each member of the backing group blew, plucked, banged, or shook their instrument as appropriate and with all their energy and fervour, whilst Goodie and Hattie sang the refrain.

The person in whose honour the song was being sung sat in his special chair, his elbow on the arm-rest, and his hand obscuring the lower part of his face. There were tears in his eyes, and a funny kind of snorting noise was coming very quietly from behind his fingers. His shoulders were slightly shaking: though whether in time to the music, or for some other reason, it was hard to tell.

Nearby sat Sacc, beaming with a mother-hen pride as she watched her chicks perform.

Behind her stood Roulus, his arms folded across his immense chest, and his head bowed so that he was having to look up at the stage from beneath his eyebrows. His lips were pressed tight together to stop them twitching and his shoulders, too, seemed to be slightly shaking though, again, for what reason you could not be sure.

St. Francis, snapping his fingers in time to the music, sat next to Sacc, with mighty Zanton lying beside him. Lamb, as ever, was curled up between his paws. On Zanton's other side was St. Peter, stroking his bristling beard as he listened, and making no attempt to hide his delighted smile.

'Jay-Cee!
O-oh Jay-cee
nothing could repla-cee
you
in
our
l-i-i-i-ives,' belted out Wideshoes.

'Yeah! Yeah! Yeah!' sang Goodie and Hattie, doing a small dance routine in perfect co-ordination with each other.

On the final line, Zanton let out a mighty roar – its sound at first overwhelming, then blending, with the music and the words.

Wideshoes swung the microphone round like a lassoo, twirled round twice – then tripped over the stand as it caught between her legs. With great presence of mind, she turned the resulting sprawl onto the stage into a dramatic conclusion to the song by kicking one leg in the air, and theatrically throwing back her head.

The audience went wild, rising to its feet, clapping and stamping and shouting, 'More! More! More!'

Wideshoes extricated herself from the microphone stand and, together with the others, took her bow.

The Theatre Company lined up for the final curtain call. One by one from the left and one by one from the right they came on, linked hands, and marched down to the front of the stage to take their bow. First, those who had played the smallest parts, then moving through to those who had had the biggest input. No one was missed out. They all took a share of the applause.

Last of all, Wideshoes entered from the left, and Goodie from the right. They met in the middle and, for a moment, stood and stared at one another.

Roulus held his breath.

Then, as if they had both reached the same decision at exactly the same second, Wideshoes grinned at Goodie and Goodie smiled at Wideshoes. Goodie held out her hand and

Wideshoes grasped it. Together, they walked down the stage to take their bow.

Roulus let out his breath in a relieved sigh, and smiled down at Sacc, who had turned to share her pleased smile with him.

Jacey also smiled, and nodded, and clapped as enthusiastically as anyone. He did not seem at all surprised – as if he had always known this would be the outcome of the rivalry between his two cherubs.

'Another extraordinary thing,' commented Roulus to Sacc, as they sat a couple of days later, talking about the Show, 'when all the different marks had been decided, and variously taken away and added on, the final result has been that Goodie and Co., and Wideshoes and Gang, have come out exactly equal.'

CHAPTER 21

Holy Night

It was five minutes to midnight on Christmas Eve. All of heaven was breath-held with expectation. As many as possible had squeezed into the Great Meeting Place, and many more were gathered around the perimeter. The whole assembly was hushed and still beneath the velvet-black sky and glittering stars.

Thousands of tiny lights of every colour of the rainbow sent their own sparkle out into the darkness. Ribbons and streamers, tinsel, garlands of flowers and many other decorations were hung from every conceivable point. No one's contribution had been rejected. A space was found for every offering, however small or simple.

It was all heart-achingly, heart-stoppingly beautiful.

Hattie sat with the other cherubs in their specially allocated place, hugging her knees. The ribbons and streamers reminded her of the first day she had arrived, and of her birthday party. Now she was at Jacey's birthday party, and everyone was dressed in their best clothes.

She thought, as she so often did, of her mum and dad, her family and friends; of them spending their first Christmas without her. Hattie said a heartfelt prayer, again as she so often did, that they would know that she was oh! so happy, that they would know how much she loved and thought about them, and that they would be happy and at peace too.

'Happy Christmas, Mum and Dad,' she whispered softly. 'I love you!'

The famous actress had, as promised, taken Hattie under her wing. Hattie adored the times they spent together, and she had already learned a great deal. The Cherub Theatre Company Show had been her first opportunity to put into practice the lessons she had been given and her teacher, who had attended, had been delighted with her.

'Darling!' she had exclaimed after the show, clasping Hattie's hands in her own. 'I was enraptured! You have such talent! It was all just too, too wonderful for words!' Hattie grinned to herself as she remembered.

Tictoc, seated next to Hattie, thought of how he had changed inside himself these last months. 'The Jacey Challenge has had a really big effect on me – actually, on all of us,' he reflected. His adventures with Peter's Expedition had been a real eye-opener. It had broadened his understanding both of himself, and of possibilities for the future.

'Actually, I've grown up a lot,' he thought, 'but there's a heap more growing to do yet.' The knowledge both pleased and excited him. And he did not mean his physical size: though, if he carried on growing at this present rate, he would be competing with Roulus one day. 'What a thought!' He looked sideways at Roulus, and grinned.

Roulus turned his head and smiled back cheerily. Exactly the same thoughts about the change in Tictoc were going through his mind, as well. In fact, he was immensely pleased and proud of all his cherubs, and of how they had all benefited in one way or another from the Jacey Challenge.

Speck sat on Tictoc's left, with his arm around Zanton, wordlessly sharing secrets with him, and absorbing the silent replies. If asked, he would probably have replied, 'I 'spect I've grown up a lot, too.'

Wishbone was one of those honoured by being chosen to play the flute tonight, and so he was seated on stage with all the other musicians. The Cherub Theatre Company Show had awoken in him a real desire to develop his great natural gift for music, and now he was determined to work hard at it. He looked up and caught Peter's eye. Peter winked, smiled and mouthed 'Hi, First Mate.' Wishbone grinned, and winked back.

Wideshoes sat on Roulus's foot as it was more comfortable than sitting on the ground. Roulus's hand rested lightly on her unusually well-brushed mop of curls. Every so often, he had been teasing her by twitching his foot suddenly and practically unseating her but, now, they both sat as silently and as still as everyone else.

Wideshoes looked at Goodie, perfectly groomed as always, standing in the front row of the choir on the stage. 'Who would've thought she 'n' me would've put on a show together,' she giggled silently. 'And become friends.'

Suddenly, the hushed quiet was broken by a great and wondrous sound of bells joyously pealing out, celebrating and proclaiming the beginning of Christmas Day, and in memory of the birth on Earth of the Saviour of the World. The musicians and the choir on stage joined in, so that a tremendous shout of praise rang out, the sounds blending and swelling until the very air seemed to throb; reaching out and embracing those present, then rolling onward and upward toward the waiting and watching stars.

Wideshoes slipped her arms round her friend's neck. 'Happy Christmas, dearest Hattie,' she said softly. Then she reached out and hugged all her special people nearby.

All around them the same scene was being repeated. Wideshoes, Hattie, Tictoc and Speck linked hands. They and Wishbone would *always* be best friends.

Much fun and laughter, some tears, and many more adventures lay ahead of them.

They would share them together.

Other titles in the series